## About the Author

Richard Britten has been an accountancy professional and seasoned commuter for many years. The endless hours of travel and commuting from the West Country to the Thames Valley led to a passion for losing himself into thriller novels of all shapes and sizes. Married with two children and a dog he now works, writes and lives in the Aberdeenshire countryside.

To Margie, Will and Timmy

Richard Britten

# THE TRUSTEE

AUSTIN MACAULEY
PUBLISHERS LTD.

A CIP catalogue record for this title is available from the British Library.

ISBN 978 1 78455 953 3 (Paperback)
ISBN 978 1 78455 955 7 (Hardback)

www.austinmacauley.com

First Published (2015)
Austin Macauley Publishers Ltd.
25 Canada Square
Canary Wharf
London
E14 5LQ

Printed and bou

# Prologue
# The Grand Hotel, St Moritz

The meeting had been long and tiresome having kicked off very early on in the morning, with the sun not even visible then over the peaks of the mountains. All three of the Trustees were there as usual together with their teams of advisers who had been pouring through business issues, the accounts and many sensitive matters of corporate strategy. By the time all outstanding items of business had been dealt with it was late on in the afternoon and a lot of people around the table were getting visibly restless, looking at their watches and stifling yawns hoping not to give themselves away.

Through the window it was still bright and crisp outside, as the curious iridescent Alpine sunshine was by now streaming into an already warm room and causing the atmosphere inside to become stifling, the attentions of most of the people in the room started drifting to more enjoyable pursuits for the weekend ahead, maybe even a chance to get some time out there on the slopes if they were lucky. Most people that is, but not all: For there was one person in that room who had only one thing on their mind as the meeting started moving to a close – and their thoughts were of coldblooded murder.

The Grand was a hotel that was always in great demand throughout the year, but this time perhaps more than most as it was the height of the skiing season. It was a luxurious hotel having a global reputation for being a playground to the rich and famous and was to be found perched high up on a mountain top in the beautiful Swiss Alps around St Moritz. The glittering clientele of celebrities and corporate rock stars would frequently be disappointed when they were unable to reserve their favourite suites, or any suite at all on occasion; such was the reputation of exclusivity that went before The Grand. But for the group of three men in that room, known only as the Trustees, ownership had its benefits and so every year they would return to The Grand to occupy the very best of the suites that the hotel had to offer.

'And so gentlemen,' concluded the pale faced man in a breathless voice, 'as we endeavour to bring The Foundation out of the past century there remains much for us to do, but above all it is vital that we weed out the old practices that we have tolerated for too long and strive to lead both commerce and governments down a road of enlightenment.' He stopped clearly drained of energy, and with a gesture of his right hand one of his aides stepped behind him easing his wheelchair away from the table.

'Very good,' said the Chairman, 'we'll draft the minutes for circulation to all three Trustees; you'll be able to retrieve these from the virtual office over the coming days – and may I also say that as we now go our separate ways how much I look forward to meeting you both again next year.' His smile suddenly froze giving way to embarrassment. Looking down at his hands he started wringing them together in discomfort realising the insensitivity of his remarks. 'Meeting adjourned!'

Paul Aldridge felt a pang of deep regret as he was wheeled from the conference room into the elegant hallway and onwards towards the lifts. Everything about the hotel spoke of opulence, from the gold leaf frieze to the luxurious deep pile of the carpet. His personal assistant who was pushing him in his wheelchair paused when they reached the end of the corridor, and having pressed the button they waited for the lift to arrive. In the silence of the moment Paul noticed that his chair was angled sideways on to the lift doors which were immediately to his right. On his left he looked at a fine example of a Louis XVI rosewood display table bearing an extravagant floral display in front of a half-length mirror. Gazing through the flowers the reflection that he saw peering back at him was almost unrecognisable – he now had hollow cheeks his features gaunt and jaundiced; so different from how he looked a year before, the tall athletically built man who despite his three score years and ten would then easily have passed as in his late fifties and cut a rather dashing figure: He knew that this would be his last meeting with his fellow Trustees – his sadness was almost overwhelming.

Paul's assistant pressed the button on the ornate panel inside the lift compartment for the eighth floor where their executive suite was located occupying almost a quarter of the entire floor of the hotel. It included a dedicated butler and maid service together with its own sauna and spa – not that it was of very much interest to the Trustee. Nevertheless as well as the Trustee the apartment housed his team as was usually the case when he travelled to Switzerland for the annual meeting of Trustees and this year they were also joined by Paul's personal physician who was to be on hand to help him cope; such was the severity of his condition.

'Are you alright, sir?' Li Wei enquired with genuine concern. His personal assistant met Paul more than forty years earlier in the most bizarre circumstances. Since then he had been a devoted servant to the Trustee and while he did tend to fuss a little too much for a proud man like Paul, the Trustee knew it was only because he cared and so was careful to resisted the urge to be too sharp with him, despite his suffering.

'Some things have to be done Li Wei,' he said in a thoughtful way and rested a friendly hand on the Asian man's arm. 'I always thought there would be more time to transform The Foundation to be the force for good that it can be. And, I must confess that I'm worried now that the other two will resist us moving from the old ways, I believe they sense a loss of power and influence – the fear of change can be a powerful force and all too often a destructive one at that.'

When the lift arrived at the eighth floor Li Wei pushed the man through an antechamber and into the elegant suite.

They were alone, the others careful of giving Paul time and space after such a long day. Li Wei pushed him towards the large picture window in the living area which overlooked the majestic mountain scenery glorious in the brightness of the early evening sunshine, shadows from the mountains to the west of them slowly marching east along the valley floor below.

'It's beautiful.' Said Paul.

'Your doctor is in the side room, sir, when you are ready,' said Li Wei as he helped the sick man into a reclining chair, leaving a glass of water on his table – no appetite for anything these days. By this time Paul was exhausted and frustrated in equal measure. There was so much that needed to be done, but he also knew that his time was running out.

'Find my heir, Li Wei, it's more important now than ever...You remember the girl don't you?'

'Yes, sir, I do; I liked her very much.'

'Find the child Li Wei,' Paul said, 'before they do.'


Everybody other than the two remaining Trustees had cleared the room as the weekend beckoned. After the annual meetings this was always a time that the Trustees would spend together, to wind down and relax a little in each other's company before they would head off on their own separate ways again. They had been meeting like this in The Grand Hotel every year for decades and had fallen into a predictable routine; old habits die hard.

The two of them moved to the other end of the wood panelled conference room where they reclined into green leather chesterfield sofas around a large coffee table next to a fireplace. Enjoying a glass of fine cognac and a Cuban cigar they found time to relax, shooting the breeze together. There would normally be three of them taking the opportunity to rebuild relationships like this, which is always important after a day of frank exchanges; but this year it was all different, the balance of power was shifting. Now it was just the big man and the Chairman left there alone at the end of the day.

'It's such a shame about Paul,' started the Chairman he's a good man you know, just like his father.

'Y—es,' drawled the big man, a tall Texan with slicked back white hair, tell-tale streaks of nicotine betraying a taste for his favourite cigars that he always treated the others to at the AGM, 'but y' know it seems to me that we're going to find ourselves at a bit of a crossroads before very long Mr Chairman – once he's gone I mean.'

After a brief pause he continued. 'I'm sorry I know that sounds a bit indelicate like, but y'know we've got to be realistic, we must think about The Foundation. And I honestly have to say that personally I don't think that this is any time to be talking about changing the way that we do things; the balance of society needs both positive *and* negative influences.' He blew out a long ribbon of blue smoke, slapping his long arms over the back of the sofa – a trail of ash falling from his cigar over the green leather.

'It's not common knowledge but there was talk of an heir sometime in the past.' Commented the Chairman. 'Of course it might just be gossip, and Paul never did marry – but he has always been very private about his personal life, so I guess it is possible. You'll appreciate that if it turns out to be true then, just as it has always been, his legacy will pass down to the next generation. Same as the rest of us ...' the Chairman wasn't able to finish his sentence as the Texan impatiently butted in, unable to keep the frustration out of his voice.

'I know I know all that stuff Chairman, but seems to me with all of his new fangled ideas an' all, that it might be sensible to contest any claim to the legacy...if one really exists which I highly doubt.' The Texan stood up and walked to the window to perch on the ledge. He continued.

'An' of course if there is no heir, then as the remaining Trustees, the constitution dictates that we have to divide Paul's segment of the Foundation to be distributed equally between us. It's for the good of continuity … if you get my meaning Mr Chairman.'

The Chairman cautiously nodded his agreement.

Finishing his cognac the Texan got up and offering his hand shook the Chairman's hand in a vice like grip.

'I have no doubt Mr Chairman that we will be in touch, I'm sure matters will develop sooner rather than later and we're gonna have to be ready to bring matters to a head – I look forward to seeing you again next year, sir.'

And with a formal nod of his head he left the room. Unlike Paul and the Chairman, the Texan had arranged to immediately leave the hotel taking the express elevator down into the private underground parking lot. A uniformed driver was already standing to attention alongside a sleek black Mercedes sedan; he held the door open as the Texan got into the car.

Within seconds they had pulled out of the hotel grounds and onto the main mountain pass. The big man wasted no time punching a series of numbers into his mobile. He knew that it was a secure line and that he could speak openly – the phone only rang once before being answered:

'Find the heir,' he barked, 'and when you find 'em … kill 'em.'

# One

The television was tuned in to the local news channel displaying a grainy image on the small, unwatched screen. The camera captured the scene of the beach at St Cyrus, twenty miles south along the rugged coastline from Aberdeen; the Silver City. Sweeping dunes fringed a vast, unoccupied beach cut off by soaring red cliffs at the far end. The weather had steadily worsened throughout the day and now as the low grey clouds had blocked out much of the remaining daylight they appeared to reach down to the horizon where they became indistinguishable from the grey sea rising up to meet them. The beach itself was unoccupied, not only because of the wind and rain driving off of a North Sea flecked with needles of sleet, but also because of the trail of blue and white plastic police tape that cordoned off all the entry points to the beach. An army of police officers and SOCOs could be seen in the background of the camera shot. They flitted in and out of the temporary structure that had been hastily erected over the corpse that had been washed up and unceremoniously dumped on the sand, where it had waited hours to be found by the early afternoon dog walker.

'...*little is known of who the victim was or how he came to meet such a tragic end.*', said the windswept reporter only just audible through the crackling on Floyd's ageing portable television set, '*... persons close to the investigation have confirmed that the body is that of a man thought to be in his* *mid to late twenties and appearing to be of eastern European origin. No identification has been made as yet, but unnamed sources have suggested that the man may have been working illegally on the North Sea which may go some way in explaining why nobody has come forward with any information for fear of prosecution or reprisals. We are expecting a formal comment from the investigating officer within the hour. In the meantime back to you Hugh in the studio ...'* The static drowned out the sound as Floyd thumped the top of the television finally giving up and heading for the sofa.

'What a pile of rubbish, not sure why I don't just replace it,' he said to himself but still deciding to leave it switched on.

His girlfriend was used to Floyd talking himself out of spending money on luxuries and he knew she could read him like a book. Not that he was ungenerous, but as a cautious man Floyd always wanted to know he was getting good value. After all he was an accountant, or at least he would be next year if he studied hard enough and got through the final examination papers – he had failed them last year and so couldn't afford to fail them again this time. Anyway, what with the wedding later in the year and the new apartment they had recently rented together, Floyd needed to save every penny.

'I think you are allowed some nice things, Handsome,' said Yvette playfully as she pecked him on the cheek while heading for the front door. With her handbag slung over her shoulder she grabbed her notepad which was on the stand by the door.

'Don't wait up for me, sweetie, it's going to be a late one tonight; I've got to get my staff at the bar ready for the function this weekend. And you know what; as usual they are so unprepared!

'Really, do you have to go in this evening?' He whined from the sofa where he reclined surrounded by text books and scribblings. He immediately regretted his tone not wanting to sound too needy.

'What I mean is that I'm not going to be at this much longer, maybe another half an hour or so. And I was thinking that maybe we could grab a takeaway and open a bottle of that plonk you brought back from Calais last week. What do you think?' There was often something special around the place after one of Yvette's trips; he had to admit it she always had great taste.

'I'd like nothing better, hon.' She often used that transatlantic way of speaking, he wasn't too sure where she had picked it up from; but he did like it.

She had his full attention by now as she smoothed her stockings drawing both of her hands up her legs, first the left and then the right, she then stepped into her shoes slipping them on effortlessly.

'But I really do have to go in tonight, babes. Larry would normally be able to cover the bar area on a Thursday night but it's the last real chance I'm going to get with this shift to do a run through – sorry.'

Floyd still needed to pinch himself when he thought about it to convince him that he wasn't dreaming. His head was still spinning at the luck of falling for a girl like Yvette ...and perhaps more to the point her falling for him. This was the real deal.

Floyd always felt that he wasn't a bad catch, but had to admit he never really had a great deal of success with girls. Yes he was reasonably good-looking to some, pretty average to most really; he was in his late twenties and already displaying a few streaks of grey making their way from his temples and over his ears. Everything else was average, safe, just what you would expect from a person choosing to make a living filling out other people's tax returns.

But, Yvette, 'oh what an English Rose', he would think to himself, with her shoulder-length dark hair, a gentle smile, steel-blue eyes and an elfin nose, she could have had her pick of the guys; it sometimes just seemed too good to be true. But true it was.

It had been such a whirlwind romance since their first encounter. But sometimes you just know when something is meant to be: right?

The first time that Floyd had met Yvette was at a charity night out with a group of friends, who were mostly couples, leaving Floyd feeling like a bit of a spare part. Floyd had recently broken up with his long term girlfriend and after a few weeks of moping around had set up a Facebook page determined to reignite his social life and telling the world about his new found freedom. And it worked, a lot of Floyd's friends, some from the distant past, rallied around him inviting him to all manner of lame events determined that he should be just the same as them.

As luck would have it Yvette had been at the same charity fundraiser that evening. She must have been with another group but during a break in the music had sat down on Floyd's table resting her feet from the dancing. As his mates pulled faces and leered at the pretty girl who was trying to strike up a conversation with him Floyd sulked embarrassed at his own coyness. It only took a little time and for the wine to carry on flowing when slowly Floyd began to lose his inhibitions. The two of them started talking like long lost buddies, engrossed in each other's company until the small hours of the morning. And as one thing led to another a second date quickly followed.

After she had left the apartment Floyd sat there lost in his thoughts, white noise from the television set the only sound. It took a few moments for him to shake himself from his reverie when it dawned on him that Yvette had forgotten to take her mobile telephone with her which he now saw on the kitchen counter – his world only just returning back into focus. He knew that her life was on that thing and she'd be lost without it; besides he always enjoyed sending her flirty texts when she was at work and even better when she sent them back. In one fluid motion Floyd launched himself over the top of the sofa and into the kitchen area where he grabbed the telephone together with his keys. Whipping quickly around he dashed through the hallway and chased after Yvette. Slamming the front door of the apartment shut behind him he took the communal stairs two or three at a time down the two floors. He'd have to be quick if he was going to catch her before she reached her car. He sprinted into the night.

'Yvie Yvie, you've forgotten your phone', he called galloping along the path towards her. Now regretting his haste as he only had socks on his feet, he needed to be careful to avoid the puddles following the earlier downpour of rain.

He could see her a hundred yards further along the road. She was now standing by her car which was in a long row of cars parked up road side for the night. Fortunately her car was also directly under a street lamp and in the yellowy tinge of its glow he could make out that she was looking for her car keys in her bag while simultaneously speaking on a telephone clutched against her ear by her bunched up shoulder. That can't be right, he figured, looking at the mobile telephone in his hand.

He called again trying to be heard over the sound of a siren wailing along the street at the far end of their road, but as he approached her she seemed wrapped up in whatever it was that she was doing and failed to acknowledge him. Gasping for breath he reached out and placed his hand on her shoulder about to make some cheeky remark.

Surprised by the unexpected touch of his hand Yvette whipped around suddenly.

'What the hell ...' she yelled her face contorted in anger, but she managed to pull herself up quickly when she saw that it was only Floyd with her telephone in his outstretched hand. Floyd was taken aback by the sheer aggression in her voice stepping backwards he held up his hands as if in mock surrender. At the moment that her head turned around to see him his mind took a snap shot of the ferocity in her expression the intensity of which shook him, it was a side to his English Rose that he had not seen before. And, as quickly as it had surfaced the shadow passed over her face and was gone. Her expression quickly replaced with the pretty angelic features he

21

knew and loved. Yvette took a step towards him and using her right arm embraced him followed by a peck on the cheek. What was unseen to Floyd was her other hand as she slipped an object quietly into her bag.

'Oh, babes, you gave me such a fright,' she gushed offering up a beaming smile, 'what's up?'

'Phone,' blurted Floyd clumsily thrown off of his guard by his girlfriend's earlier reaction, 'I mean your mobile ... I spotted it on the counter just after you left and, well, I thought you might need it – so here I am, with it.'

'Oh you're such an angel, hon, thanks for that, where would I be without my knight in shining armour?' She teased him. 'I'll try not to wake you when I get in – or perhaps you'd like me to?' She cooed tilting her head to one side pouting like a French model.

'Why, Miss Semple, I do believe you are flirting with me.' Floyd quipped trying to compose himself, 'Catch you later.'

As he walked back to the apartment along Union Grove he could hear the sound of her sports car turning onto St Swithin Street and accelerating away rapidly. It was quieter now and in a moment of solitude Floyd briefly considered just getting his coat and shoes and heading off to the nearest sports bar for a couple of beers and some company.

Unsettled by the last five minutes Floyd replayed the events in his mind wondering what it was that she had slipped into her bag. He had a growing sense that whatever it was he was not meant to see it, and whether it was possible to really know somebody.


Back at the apartment Floyd absent-mindedly flicked though his study notes but had lost the focus and the desire to do any more.

'OK then, let's see if I can get this thing working again' he mumbled switching on the old television set and readjusting the aerial, pointing it this way and that until a reasonable picture scrolled down the screen. Satisfied with the result Floyd flicked though the channels hoping for something light-hearted and funny to pick up his mood. Having made a brew he sat back down and watched a stern-looking senior police officer speaking into a microphone as he answered a reporter's question. Floyd could just about make out the name at the bottom of the screen introducing Assistant Chief Constable Scott Cooper.

Sod it where is that remote? He thought to himself taking an age to find it wedged behind the sofa cushion. Pointing it at the television Floyd turned the volume up.

'...and so we are appealing to the public for any information no matter how insignificant they feel it is to call this number....' the shot panned back to the reporter. Floyd recognised her from the earlier windswept scene on St Cyrus beach. She had since had time to recompose herself and apply a fresh coat of lippy.

'... and so there we have it; police remain baffled by the appearance of a man's body which was swept up on the beach at St Cyrus in Aberdeenshire earlier today. And while very little is being released at this time the Police have provided some details about the man who apparently has a distinguishing scar on the back of his upper leg.

'Conditions have been atrocious here and difficult for the scenes of crime officers to gather any meaningful forensic information. And while the cause of death is unknown the police are hopeful of gaining more insights following the post mortem examination. Hugh ...'

Floyd sipped his tea and as he waited for it to cool down idly flicking through his emails on his new iPhone deleting much of the rubbish in the process. 'So much crap, where on earth does it all come from,' he muttered to himself. He'd spent hours setting up his new toy, amazed at how much technology had progressed but now finding that with it comes a tidal wave of spam – everybody trying to part you from your hard earned cash, he thought. But not one to look a gift horse in the mouth Floyd was made up when he won the phone in the tombola at the charity evening – he figured it must be a sign that his luck was turning. A great night all round.

It had been a long and even a little bit of a weird day. But relaxing in front of the box a sense of contentment and weariness eventually caught up with him. He gave in and headed off to bed early to get some sleep. 'Hope she does wake me up,' he said to himself as he drifted off, 'you're a lucky guy Floyd Carter!'

# Two

Becca woke up a few minutes before the alarm was set to go off at 5.30 a.m. as she wanted to get a head start on the day.

Turning on the bedside lamp she absorbed her surroundings – the contemporary décor of the hotel room that she had checked into yesterday afternoon was clean and chic. Reaching out she switched off the alarm avoiding by seconds the brash buzzing from her travel clock. The hotel was adjacent to the railway station and a convenient base to dump her luggage and camera equipment before venturing out for a bite to eat and perhaps a few drinks. That was yesterday, today as she gained control of her senses she couldn't remember the name of the naked body lying in the bed next to her.

'Hey,' she nudged his inert frame with her elbow.

'What was that stuff you were plying me with last night after we got back from the Vault? My throat feels like a sandpit.'

He grunted and fidgeted not nearly ready to awaken. Becca gazed down at the intricate tattoos reaching up his muscular torso stretching up around his neck and under his chin. Like Becca her pick-up was also adorned with dozens of body piercings. She zoned out and found herself lazily tracing her fingers along the serpent surrounding his hips.

'Well since you are here and I have absolutely no intention of ever seeing you again,' she said, 'you had better put yourself to good use.' He pretended not to hear – sleep was desperately needed following a crazy night of too much booze, too much of everything, with that creature. Man she was crazy, bold as brass she had walked over to him in the Vault right in front of all of his crowd and told him she enjoyed getting an eyeful of his body art and 'what does a girl have to do to get a private viewing?' Clad in black leather with her midriff showing her own ink and piercings he was putty in her hands.

'You know, stud, I've been working through my own particular addiction with my therapist,' she whispered in his ear, 'but after last night I think this little trip might have set me back a bit and I blame you entirely.'

Pick-up's face knotted into a frown: 'What the hell are you on about, it was only booze last night, a shitload of booze right enough, but that's all, I didn't slip anything else into your glass.' He protested wearily.

'It's not what you slipped into my glass that I'm talking about.' She teased. 'It's a different type of addiction altogether.' Becca purred as she took matters into her own hands giving over to that primitive part of her being, her lizard brain – just feeling not thinking. What's to think about anyway, she reckoned.


Living mostly with her mother for much of her childhood Becca had the charmed existence of the middle classes, cared for by her parents inhabiting a world of quintessential Englishness. Her father had worked and lived in London throughout the working week which left little chance for her to spend time with him during those early years, but she loved him dearly all the same and was always so excited to greet him off the train in Pewsey on a Friday evening. Her father, working as an editor for all of those years, had given Becca her taste for journalism. She would sit down with him at the kitchen table late on a Friday evening bursting with excitement in a way that only children can, running through her latest contribution to whatever school newspaper was going, hanging on his every word and expression – for these are the moments that she cherished and lived for.

But sometimes life can be cruel and when her father was taken from them by a stroke it was just Becca and her mother left to cope in that big old house in Marlborough. She and her mother, Gilly, were well provided for under the terms of her late father's will, and eventually as the months passed by they gradually emerged from their grieving settling into their gentle routine and lifestyle. As a normal life resumed Becca increasingly immersed herself in her studies at the local comprehensive school that she now attended at the top of the hill; she would always enjoy her daily walk along the historic High Street, past estate agents, shop windows displaying all manner of curios and the local Waitrose store – this was truly the home for the comfortable Wiltshire set.

Throughout her teenage years Becca was often slow to make friends and never saw life as a popularity contest the way some do. Not that she was anti-social or lacking any of the normal social skills for getting on with her classmates. Indeed as girl gave way to young lady she attracted more and more attention from various admirers. Simply life was just easier by not trying too hard to break into those school yard cliques: Naturally introverted, while Becca had only a few friends, they were good friends – she knew them and they knew her and they could talk about anything: Especially Floyd.

Even now when she thought of him she recalled the long hours that they would spend together listening to each other's music in the downstairs play room. She still had the compilation tape that Floyd made up for her shortly after they had first met sharing as they did a similar taste in music like The Manic Street Preachers, Robbie Williams and Fatboy Slim.

Back then Floyd had been quite a shy teenager, he had a nice family and while they were very different from Becca's own family, being of a working class background, she liked them very much. His mother worked part time to help ends meet also balancing the needs of the growing family while his father worked for many years in a car factory in Swindon. The Carter family lived on the council estate on the northern side of town so Floyd would always prefer to cycle over to Becca's when they planned to hang out enjoying the view over The Green, the character of the Atworths' beautiful old townhouse with its timber beams and flagstone floors, and the peel of the bells as the bell ringers would practice their chorus every Thursday evening. This was her life throughout her school years until she recalled that day that they were sitting together in her playroom during the Easter holidays.

'Becca, I've got something to tell you.' He said, clearly looking for the words.

'Go on, Floyd, just spit it out. What's the problem?'

'Well you know that my Dad lost his job last October with the last round of redundancies at the factory.'

'Go on.' She encouraged, sensing his discomfort.

'Well he's got a new job.'

'Oh that's great news, Floyd, I am so happy for you all.'

'Ye—es, I guess, but you see Dad has had to retrain to get a new job and, well even though he's still working as a fabricator he won't be working in car production any more. For his new job he's going to be working for a company that makes accommodation units for oil rigs and things like that – and for him to be able to do that then he has to move away. And you see his new job is based near Aberdeen.'

Becca knew Aberdeen was in Scotland but quite where she wasn't certain.

'So does this mean that you will only see your Dad on the weekends 'cos I still remember what that was like with my Dad – I guess it can work but it can be difficult, too. I know you and your Dad are close.'

'No Beccs you're missing the point. Dad is going up there next week, he's got a place to stay that the company have organised, but while he's there he'll also be looking for a

28

house to rent and, well, once that's sorted we're all going up there … to live.'

Becca was stunned and sat there shell shocked into silence. Floyd was her best friend, her soul mate and she was losing him; first her father now Floyd. Words failed her as she drew him close to her embracing him as she nestled her face under his chin embarrassed at the tears that escaped her. In the background Robbie Williams sang a song of Angels.


Stepping into the shower Becca turn the settings randomly and shuddered in surprise as the chilly water suddenly cascaded over her, causing her to beat a hasty retreat out of the cubicle.

'Why on earth do they always make these taps so bloody complicated.' She cursed some more as she yanked the thermostat in the opposite direction instantly scolding her hand which was upturned testing the water.

'Come on Goldilocks, not too hot and not too cold … that's it,' she murmured returning to the cubicle. She stood there face up to the out pouring of water cleansing her, happy to be on her own once again having ejected pick-up from her room never to be seen again.

'Can't keep doing this, sweetheart,' she reproached herself as the afterglow or her carnal activities waned to be replaced by that old familiar self-loathing an aching in the pit of her stomach leaving her feeling dirty – she scrubbed her skin relentlessly until it was red raw – seeking whatever cleansing could be found there.

As she pulled herself together she reckoned that the only way forward was to throw herself into the day's activity and by seven thirty she was sitting in the hotel restaurant picking through a large cooked breakfast replenishing her energy reserves. In front of her a folder full of names, places and a timeline, an overview of the investigation that she had been pulling together for months – and now this latest development.

Well, if I'm lucky enough, she thought, I may get something from the pathology staff. She had been given a heads up that the post mortem was to be carried out this morning; it seemed that the police were pulling out all of the stops on this one. She knew that there was more to it and with a fair wind she would be able to bust this wide open.

'Another coffee, please, over here.' She waved at the waitress trying to get her attention. The petite waitress shimmied over looking more than a little intimidated by Becca's dark black eye liner, lip stick and ensemble in black.

'Sorry, madam, is everything okay?' The young waitress enquired.

'Yes just peachy – put another coffee in there would you? Becca instructed nudging her mug forward.

'Oh, and by the way, are you from around here?' she enquired.

'Yes, well from the North East, moved into town a couple of years ago, why's that?'

'No reason really, well no actually that's a lie, you see I'm a journalist,' she lied, 'and I'm currently doing some research into – well that doesn't really matter – but what I would like to do is interview some of Aberdeen's working girls, if you know what I mean, and I'm guessing that there's an area where they normally go to ply their trade – right?' Her inflection indicating a question.

The name-tag on the waitress's lapel told Becca that her name was Mhairi.

'Sorry, Mhairi, didn't mean to put you on the spot.'

'No that's OK.' Mhairi composed herself, topping Becca's mug with fresh coffee.

'You're right there seems to be a lot of that type of activity here. You know Aberdeen is a real boom town at the moment and there are lots of guys from all over the world working in the oil with plenty of cash burning a hole in their pockets. You know how it is.' Becca knew.

'Anyway take a trip down Market Street which runs along the side of the harbour and down the Quays after about six or seven o'clock in the evenings – you'll soon find what you're looking for.'

'Thanks, Mhairi.' Becca purred giving her a flirtatious wink.

'See you around maybe?'

Mhairi spun on her heels catching the eye of another hungry guest to help.

# Three

Marek was late again; damn him, he was supposed to be here before six and it was a bitterly cold morning. Not one for idly waiting around. Si paced up and down outside the lock up fingering the Beretta under his coat giving him that buzz of power and control.

'God dammit I'm gonna put a bullet in his fucking skull if he screws up like this again.' He cursed – there's plenty more where he came from.

The white Luton van drove through the gate and into the lock up yard. Around the perimeter of the yard was an eight foot high prefabricated concrete slab wall which was ideal for keeping out any unwanted attention and prying eyes.

'Quick over here you useless piece of shit – get the cargo into the holding pen.'

Marek knew he would be in trouble if he faltered, of course he couldn't help being late – problems on the crossing from Calais but he knew that wouldn't wash with Si – better to say nothing than to risk punishment like last time. Pushing up the metal roller door with a clatter Marek entered the back of the van. With a heave he pushed one, and then the other metal wire cages onto the hydraulic tailgate. Reaching for the controller he pressed the green button to lower the cargo down to ground level.

Best not to look, Marek thought, just do the job and get the cages into the bay while you still have all of your limbs intact.

'That's me all done, Si, guess I'll be off now.'

'Don't piss me about like this again Marek, now fuck off and next time you get the call be on time.' Marek didn't need telling twice, getting into the van he peeled out of the yard and was away.

Peace at last. At forty seven years of age Si felt he was getting more philosophical about life – you have to let yourself enjoy your work was his motto – and he did, and this was the bit that he enjoyed best.

He liked to be called Si, allowing people to assume his name was Simon, or Simeon, but it was neither. Born Silvije Petrovic in the suburbs of Zagreb, Si became an enthusiastic militiaman during the nineties conflict in the former Yugoslavia – his particular skills and temperament were greatly prized by certain leaders in those days. But of course that was then. It was all about "us and them" back then – now it's just about business and of course using his God given talents.

Sealing the outer door, he made certain that the sound proofing fell back into place and the blackouts were properly intact. Satisfied with his preparations, Si hovered over the cages containing the latest consignment, enjoying the anticipation of the job ahead of him.

'Well, ladies, it's time for your first lesson in compliance.'

Si was an expert, he knew all too well that while they would struggle now, after shooting them up with heroin for a couple of weeks, gradually increasing the dosage, it wouldn't take long for them to become completely hooked. When they were, there would be nothing that they wouldn't do for their next fix.

'I've got a couple of cash buyers waiting for you at the end of the month and I want you looking just fine, after all it is only business.' A thin smile slid across his face in the darkness. The grin of a predator.

'Now, who first?'

# Four

The problem with a great weekend is that there is always a Monday morning that follows it. No matter how hard he wished when he opened his eyes he knew that he would still be there in his cubicle, the cursor on his timesheet winking at him, demanding his attention.

Floyd made an effort to focus. What on earth did I do all week last week, he fretted, gazing at the holes in his total hours worked schedule. As an associate at Baker Smith & Clarkwell, a chartered accountancy firm in the centre of the city, it was time that the firm sold to their clients. Like other associates in the firm he was expected to meet a target of spending eighty percent of his working day doing work that can be billed on to those clients, or put another way at least thirty hours over the course of last week. Floyd was struggling to even find twelve hours and knew that he would be getting the wrong kind of attention from the guys upstairs if he couldn't make the cut.

Deciding it was time for a break he stepped out of his cubicle heading for the coffee machine located at the far end of the office; it was always a good excuse to stretch his legs. The tax department was only one of a number, the firm provided a range of business services to clients from bookkeeping, auditing to corporate work and tax return preparation – which was where Floyd fitted in.

It was mid-morning and the office was busy. Most of his colleagues, like Floyd, were trying to keep their heads down to look like they were busy. Others huddled in offices or conference rooms with various managers and partners. As often as not they were carrying out some form of character assassination, or empire building; at least this was what Floyd figured as he made his way along the corridor.

'Morning Archie.' He greeted his colleague in the adjacent cubicle on his return, balancing his mug of coffee in one hand and a generous slice of carrot cake in the other. 'D'you have a good weekend?'

'Aye, 'twas awesome Floyd. You know Duggie in IT, well I went out with him and his pal Daz t' watch the game at Pittodrie. The match was shite like but spent the rest o' the day working us way through the bars behind Union Street. Casino later on – all got a bit messy after that. What's it they say … I'm livin the dream right? … D'you hae a good un?'

'Not bad,' he responded automatically, but Floyd's attention had now drifted back to his carrot cake, which he was hacking into pieces with a plastic fork.

His cubicle was about four feet long and four wide. Underneath his desk was a small credenza to store a few office supplies but very little space for anything else. His cube was identical to dozens of others all housed in a modern office extension and bathed in artificial light any time of the day or night. In a day and age of digital technology Floyd was always amazed at the amount of paper and files needed, so with a computer screen and half a dozen working papers fighting for space on his desk it was constantly crowded and untidy. Battling to find a level surface for the coffee and carrot cake while chatting with Archie he happened to nudge the mouse waking up the computer monitor.

There was his timesheet still mocking him, but as well as that he also noticed the little blue box in the right hand corner of the screen which was slowly fading away telling Floyd that he had just received new email. One of many, he thought, couldn't keep on top of them. Not having properly seen the title shown on the legend he would normally have allowed himself the luxury of going through the gory details of Archie's Saturday night antics, but the subconscious part of his brain had processed something unseen, and while he didn't know why, there was something that was snagging in his mind and as he motioned the pointer on his screen using the mouse he felt pierced by a spike of anxiety, a feeling of the ground beneath his feet giving way – a premonition perhaps?

He launched the email program and scrolled to the top of his inbox. Forty seven messages unread!

Exasperated at the onslaught of email traffic he found the latest email received, ignoring the rest for the time being. The title given to the email was: *You need to see this!* Sender: *A friend.*

Floyd exhaled heavily letting his anxiety deflate with his breathing.

'Just spam,' he said under his breath to nobody in particular. 'Probably from My Dearest in Nigeria.'

'Get a grip Carter, you're getting paranoid and uptight like a coiled spring – too much coffee perhaps.'

'Need to get laid more like,' came Archie's voice from the other side of the partition. Floyd blushed realising he'd been talking to himself.

But his antennae were still bristling, his internal senses telling him there was more to it than just spam … Click, he opened the email.

Nothing.

He scrolled further down the page to find a hyperlink three lines long underlined and in blue. There was no way he was going to click on that. It wasn't long ago there was all that gossip about one of the supervisors getting canned for looking at internet porn sites on his computer during his lunch hour. Seems the firm runs some sort of Big Brother nanny software – it would be just his luck to follow a link that took him to some salacious website then to get hauled up in front of HR for a dressing down.

Scrolling further down the email he saw the final line of script which read simply – *Floyd, if you are who I think you are, then you need to see this.*

# Five

At the same time back in their second floor apartment on Union Grove Yvette was lounging on the sofa shrouded in her fleecy robe. She was indulging herself with a slow start to the day following a frantic weekend of corporate hospitality and organising an army of hotel staff – as always it ran like clockwork. The bridal party was delighted.

She pulled the flash drive out of the USB port on Floyd's lap top computer that she had ledged on her lap and then took a few moments to power down the machine. She slid the computer back into its place under the coffee table careful to ensure it was precisely where she had found it. As she gathered together her cup and plate she brushed up a handful of crumbs, the only evidence of the buttered croissant that was swiftly devoured. Yvette treasured these moments of solitude, a high achieving perfectionist her life was all too often dominated by others demanding her attentions and instruction. So, times such as these after a good job done were her chance to recharge and regroup. And besides, she wanted to get her mind into what it was that she was really here for.

Having loaded the dishwasher and ensured the kitchen was as it should be she made her way through to the bedroom and into the attaching bathroom. Just enough time for a lazy soak in the tub before her early afternoon appointment with the group accountant. Just the usual quarterly briefing to keep the bean counters happy.

Lunch was a light affair today; she had arranged to sit in the conservatory area of the hotel restaurant, bright and colourful, surrounded by luscious greenery and vivid floral displays. As acting manager of the hotel, Yvette knew the company accountant, Hans de Groot, very well and worked hard at maintaining a friendly and relaxed rapport with him – best to keep him on side she thought. As a recent newcomer to the hospitality organisation her direct superiors spotted an opportunity for her to step into a vacant position in the Aberdeen hotel following the recent departure of the previous manager under a cloud. The timing was perfect. Yvette made it her business to be well networked particularly in the Rotterdam headquarters. After all that is where all of the influence was in getting what she wanted and, if she played her cards right, she was close to getting just that.

The organisation that owned the wider global business was called The Foundation. It was a highly compartmentalised structure which valued privacy above everything else. Each segment of the organisation was run as a standalone company, the shares being held in a blind trust in Luxembourg – ensuring both segmentation and control. Unlike Yvette, Hans only worked for the hospitality business unaware of the existence of any of the Trustees, who ultimately owned The Foundation, and their wider business interests.

Yvette, on the other hand was first involved with The Foundation a number of years earlier proving her worth on a variety of highly sensitive cases. She had recently been contacted again by the man who discovered her all those years ago, and for him to contact her directly then it must be an important assignment. She had only ever seen him once and that was the first and last time that they had met, but she would never forget him with his deep rich Texan accent. The new job was particularly important and he wouldn't leave it to anybody else demanding that she heads up the Aberdeen operation. He would make the arrangements to ensure a suitable vacancy arose. After all she had her own reasons and it may well be that she could improve the flagging fortunes of their other investments in that corner of the world, too.

'So Yvette you have made a really good start of changing this ugly duckling into a beautiful swan.' He joked with her.

'Thanks Hans,' she said, 'I've had a lot of help.'

'The results against all of the desired performance indicators are really impressive. This will certainly stand you in good stead with the divisional board.' He complimented her as he placed his order with the waitress who came over to their table to take their order.

'As you know we have been conducting an internal audit over the whole of the hospitality division. It seems that somebody up top is hoping to carry out a global review, but I do not know to what end.' He paused waiting to make eye contact with Yvette who was now giving the waitress her own order.

'Sorry.' She said. 'Please do go on.'

'Well, your hotel was not originally scheduled for review until next year but I'm coming under pressure to bring as many reviews forward as possible so I think it might make sense to accelerate this one. I'll review the project when I get back to Rotterdam next week, but there is probably no reason not to commence in the next month or so.' He speared his salad with his fork as he spoke.

'What will the review involve?' Yvette quizzed him, her brow furrowing.

'Nothing to worry about I'm sure. I'll get Dimpney to send you a checklist of some of the areas that they will concentrate on. As you know we are becoming increasingly international and so I think a lot of our cross border transactions should get a degree of scrutiny. We want to be seen as good corporate citizens right? You know, none of the smoke and mirrors that we read about in the press headlines. I think there will be a detailed payroll review too, probably also checking work permits and migrant status and so on – it is the nature of this industry to have a lot of overseas workers you know.'

'Thanks for the heads up, Hans, we'll make sure that all of the necessary paperwork is in good order, make sure this duckling gets a clean bill of health'.

'I'll drink to that.' Toasted Hans with his wine glass full of Pellagrino.

They finished lunch making small talk then said their goodbyes air kissing cheeks as they parted company. Hans was keen to catch the three fifteen train to Edinburgh in order to visit their flagship Hotel in the nation's capital the following morning.

With her own mind now racing Yvette made her way to her office in the management suite on the third floor.

She took a seat behind her desk and took three or four deep breaths trying to control the rising sense of frustration and anger – she thought she would have a lot more time. Grabbing a tumbler from the antique cherry wood cabinet she poured herself a generous measure of Glenfarclas 17 year old whisky and drained it in a single mouthful.

Yvette knew that she had done a good job with the hotel, increased occupancy, per capita spending had improved dramatically while at the same time considerably reducing overheads. Of course one of the major costs of running a hotel is the cost of wages paid to staff and it was by taking advantage of The Foundations other operations that she had been able to cut wage costs dramatically.

Let's just hope I can paper over the cracks long enough on this one. All I need now is enough time, she thought all too aware of what was at stake.

As the spirits hit her belly the warmth was instant bringing down a comforting veil over her, helping to release the tension from across her shoulders. Yvette could hold her booze well, better than most men in fact. And after another quick shot she pulled herself together gathering her senses – she knew what she had to do. She fished around in the pocket of her jacket which was slung over the back of her office chair and pulled out her other mobile telephone. Hitting the contacts App she scrolled to the particular name that she was looking for and pressed dial.

It rang a few times before it was picked up.

Swivelling towards the window in her leather-backed chair she leaned forward now focussed and business-like.

'Si, it's me ... we need to talk!'

# Six

For an autumn day in Aberdeen it was surprisingly bright, the vivid colours of the last leaves on the trees uplifting as Floyd absent mindedly wandered down St Swithin Street heading back towards their apartment. While it is considered to be a city, Aberdeen is surprisingly compact and so, providing you weren't trying to get somewhere on four wheels, then nowhere is particularly far away. It was lunchtime and if it was a choice between trying to play nicely with the other guys in the office break out area, or getting the peace and solitude in his own space, Floyd would opt for the latter whenever time would allow. Besides his curiosity had been piqued by the morning's events; unable to find out more about the mystery message sent to his works email address he had forwarded it on to his own email account which he wanted to pick up, to see what else he could find out.

Entering into the apartment he filled the kettle and pulled the foil lid from the top of the Pot Noodle that he had left on the counter that morning. Reaching down he pulled his lap top out from underneath the coffee table and powered it up giving it a few minutes to go through its start up routine. In the meantime, he decided to check his phone messages while simultaneously squeezing the mango chutney sachet into his noodles. 'Floyd my boy, you're a culinary genius – Yvette would be proud of you.'

Beep, you have one new message – 'Hello, Floyd, is that you, it's Mum here, oh you know I don't like talking to these things, are you there? No, well just thought I'd call you since you have obviously lost my telephone number. Well I found out this morning ...'

Floyd zoned out and pressed the button deleting the message. 'I'll call you later, Mum.' He said to the machine.

Pressing the mail receive button he waited a few moments while half a dozen emails downloaded automatically into his inbox. Floyd immediately spotted the one from his work address. Click – there it is. Now let's see what this is all about.

Moments later the web browser presented a drop box containing a single jpg. file – a photograph. While the picture was of poor quality it was clear what the two people were doing – some might call it making love, but to Floyd's eye, however, it didn't appear that there was much love involved, instead a scene of dominance, pain and control – the young man bound, gagged and even in such a grainy image appearing to be in great distress. The female, a platinum blond, relishing the control and highly sexually charged, was biting hard on the man's ear; his body was peppered with searing bite marks and angry scratch wounds. In her left hand the glint of hard steel and a visibly sharp tip poised.

It could have been seconds or it could have been minutes. Floyd just stared at the image barely managing to control the bile rising in his throat. His first thought was that he should go to the police, but would they take him seriously? I mean, it's a still photograph and while it was a deeply disturbing image there was no indication that a crime had been committed. He closed the file and then clicked back to the email.

*Floyd you need to see this.* This is personal, he thought, I mean they use my name. Scrolling to the top of the email he examined the sender's email address to see if this would yield up any clues on who *they* were – *watchingoutforyou@gmail.com*

So nothing much to go on there he figured as he scrolled all the way down to the bottom of the message. Here there were just the usual series of characters and digits that only mean something to other computers and IT technicians.

To hell with it he thought shutting down the email but deciding not to delete it just yet.

Back in the office Floyd lifted the phone and punched in four digits. After a couple of rings the phone was lifted.

'Hi Floyd, Duggie here, how's it hanging, shame you couldn't join us on the weekend.'

'Yeah well you know how it is; Yvie was putting the shoulder in at the hotel so I had some errands to run and before you say it, yes I do know that I am completely under the thumb ... but what a thumb eh?' He said self-deprecatingly.

'But look, Duggie, that's not what I'm calling about. Thing is that I received this rather curious email which has been sent to me and I have no idea where it's come from, but you'll know how to figure that out won't you?'

'Might take me a little while to check out the IP address then to cross check it against the server's location ... but I guess you're probably not interested in that. Look, mate, can you send the email to me at home and I'll get round to it when I can, I'm up to my ears at the moment with the new office management system upgrade so I'll be burning the midnight oil here I'm afraid.'

'I appreciate that, Duggie, just when you can ok.' Floyd quickly detached the photograph attachment and after a couple of minutes looking around for Duggie's home email address typed it in and pinged it out to him.

It was one of those rare afternoons when Floyd was actually able to get stuck into his caseload at work compiling a good number of his outstanding tax returns for his clients. He also got around to following up on various queries with the Taxman and making a half decent dent in the constant email traffic that plagued his inbox.

Checking his iPhone he retrieved a further voice mail. It was a follow up call from his Mother, she probably figured on calling his mobile, too.

'I forgot to mention, darling; I'm going to be away this weekend so no need to call me. It's ever so exciting as there is an alumni do back in Marlborough and I thought; what the hell let's do it.

'I'm heading over there with Doris, she has been good enough to let me stay with her. Do you remember her, dear? She and I used to work together in the school administration office. Any way call me next week will you …?'

'Yes Mum, no Mum, three bags full Mum.' He raised his eyebrows to the ceiling. But the truth be told he loved her dearly. He smiled.

# Seven

Oksana thought that it would not be possible to suffer any more than she had already. But she was shortly about to realise just how wrong she was.

At sixteen years she was just completing her grade 10 in level three which had been a breeze. A talented student with a particular skill at modern languages she was destined for further studies at the University of Kiev. She was a popular kid at school taking part in the athletics squad and getting involved in all areas of school life.

A mature girl a couple of inches taller than most of her school mates she cut a striking figure, and while, like any teenager, she enjoyed the company of her friends almost better than anything else, she was thrilled that her mother and father decided on the family holiday to Dubrovnik in the summer. On the southern fringes of the Croatian Riviera to Oksana it seemed like a little taste of paradise.

But that would have been a couple of months ago. She had lost track of time, her real life seeming like a dream now giving way to this nightmare. Her memories since then were of long tracts of time in isolation travelling, bound and caged like an animal, the fearful terror her constant companion a surge of adrenaline every time the container was opened, screaming to fight, fright and flight – but there was nowhere for her to go.

Eventually it would become hard to remember the details of her captivity: But that night she will remember for the rest of her days; however long that might be.

Dubrovnik – August

Three days of sun, sea and sand, it was just fabulous to be away from everything. And a great chance to brush up on her languages. In addition to Ukrainian and Russian, Oksana could also speak near perfect German, good French and English and could get by quite well in Italian. So it seemed that this was the perfect place to practice most of her languages, especially English.

Having relaxed for three days Oksana pleaded with her parents to let her explore on her own that night and maybe go to a club. While they were not too happy about the idea they were swayed as she had agreed to hook up with a girl friend she had made along the corridor. Promising to look out for each other and be back by one o'clock in the morning, her parents gave in wanting her to have a great holiday.

Chatting and laughing with her new friend her parents wave goodbye to the two girls who were joking and enjoying the possibilities of the evening ahead. As they rounded the corner Oksana couldn't be happier, it wasn't even seven in the evening … they were going to have a great time.

'So where to first, Liv; food, or how about a cocktail?' She questioned in a sing song voice. Staring at Liv she was confused. She was expecting to see a bubbly smiling face but instead all she saw was a hostile grimace frozen as if time had stood still. It only took ten seconds after Liv banged the side of the large white van that they were standing beside. Immediately the rear door clattered up and He jumped down. That was the first time she had seen him – bald-shaven head, a sharp Slavic-featured face and while he was clearly middle age possessed a taut wiry frame covered by a cropped brown tee shirt, his trousers were combat fatigues together with black military boots.

Without hesitation he sucker punched her in the middle of her torso. Immediately lifting her off of her feet and expertly throwing her into the rear of the truck.

The pain was excruciating like nothing she had ever experienced before in her life. Bent in two Oksana desperately tried to draw breath, stars forming around the periphery of her vision. At that point a cloth bag was savagely thrust over her head followed by a sharp stinging in her neck – darkness fell.

It was ten minutes to seven in the evening, precisely another six hours and ten minutes until she was expected back at the apartment – and a whole twelve hours before her distraught parents would be taken seriously enough by the local police that she was missing.


She had never been to Scotland before let alone Aberdeen. Since that day in July Oksana had lost two stone in weight, had been beaten on multiple occasions, but her tormentors were always careful not to damage the goods. Having had many years of experience in inflicting pain without lasting injury – they were true experts.

But it was no longer the beating that horrified her so much as the hours after the highs that she would experience when they injected her. Her dependence was complete, and while they would carefully increase her dosage they would occasionally prolong the periods in between fixes to give her the full taste of the agony of withdrawal; its tight grip digging deeper into her soul, clammy, her insides cramping, unable to function just wanting an end. And then he would come to embrace her, to soothe her and give her what she needed now more than anything – her next hit.

# Eight

Becca hated taking no for an answer, but then rarely had she encountered such a curmudgeonly figure as Flo McGinley who, judging from the leathery features and skeletal frame, couldn't have been a day under eighty. More like a hundred thought Becca.

'Well if he does become available for comment.' she retorted to Flo, 'here's my card. It will definitely be in his interests to come forward to make a comment to the public – after all it is in the public interest you know.' She quipped referring to George MacFarlane the region's chief pathologist.

Flo sneered making a point of carelessly tossing the card into the paper tray.

She knew it would be impossible to get an audience with MacFarlane after all, as far as he, and Flo, were concerned she was just another freelance hack from Edinburgh angling for the inside line. She was of course nothing of the sort, but as a cover it was perfect to gloss over many of the activities that her true office demanded of her. As an operative in Unit 45, a shady government agency affectionately known by the few as Athena, her mission ran far deeper than MacFarlane could possibly have guessed – he was, however, going to find out and probably the hard way.

Unit 45 came into being after the Second World War but before the cold war took hold with the Eastern Bloc. At that time the Unit comprised a collection of top level intelligence analysts. However, as the Iron Curtain closed down on Europe, Athena's activities and reach deepened gaining a firm mandate from the very highest levels of the Government to operate in those dark and shady corners that others seek to avoid and to eliminate problems absolutely and with extreme prejudice – no questions asked! The Unit was in effect being run with an off-the-books budget and an autonomous directive; it was simply above the law. This was never a problem, no protests, no select committee hearings, no questions – nobody knew about Athena because – to everyone other than the few – it simply didn't exist. And just like Athena, the Greek god of war, who was the last solution in the face of a dogmatic and pedantic authority, Zeus. The Unit mirrored their Greek mythological counterpart – Athena didn't care for rules – they didn't have to.

As the years passed by following Floyd and his family's departure from Marlborough, Becca sat and aced the entrance examinations to read English literature and commenced her college years among the dreaming spires of Oxford.

Becca loved the emotional journey taken through the medieval, the eighteen century and the romantic poets: a model student. She also threw herself with abandon into everything that university life had to offer. She wrote prolifically for the Union rag, and later, as Editor, lived life from one adrenaline charged deadline to the next. Becca always had a big impact on anybody whose orbit passed through her gravitational field.

For a girl of striking looks and the charisma that she possessed it was perhaps surprising that she had only ever had one sexual encounter before Oxford. The second time happened during fresher's week tumbling drunkenly into bed with a ruddy-faced young Welshman. Others followed in quick succession during that term as she opened the floodgates on her appetite, awakening the giant that had taken residence inside her: a giant that was to become an unstoppable titan. Becca had always been a force of nature and she saw no reason to deny who she was. During her university years her sexual partners where numerous; swinging both ways she relished the great diversity in humanity. And it was while in the embrace of Shelagh Jamieson, a vivacious middle-aged visiting professor from Harvard and descendent from Irish immigrants, that she was first introduced to the world of British Secret Intelligence Services.

Not surprisingly Becca rose rapidly through the world of MI6 and had been observed with interest from a distance as a motivated operative prepared to do whatever was needed to get the result. By the time she was twenty five she had left MI6; all of her case records were erased and no trail remained of her ever stepping foot in Vauxhall Cross. As far as the world was concerned she was just another press hack.


MacFarlane eased along the North Deeside Road, traffic was still heavy at this time in the evening. Being autumn it had been dark for hours and as the rain lashed against the windscreen of his car he reflected on the events of the day. He indicated and then turned right onto Kirk Brae pulling up the hill and away from the traffic. Certainly a nice part of town, however following the economic train wreck that is divorce he now lived in a modest three bed semi. Still he kept the Jag for old times' sake which soothed him fleetingly.

Kicking the front door closed behind him he tossed his leather briefcase into the corner of the hallway on top of the assortment of shoes and boxes, he then stepped into the living room. Switching on the light he had intended to pour a measure of whisky to enjoy, but stood rigid at the sight of the young woman sat in the chair opposite. He had seen enough movies to realise that it was a silencer that she was screwing onto the end of a pistol.

Pointing the weapon at him and twitching it she motioned him to sit in the chair alongside.

'We're going to have a little chat, Doctor, and you are going to answer all of my questions. Here, let me pour that for you, I think it might help.' She half-filled his tumbler from the decanter giving him time to navigate the glass to his lips with a trembling hand, emptying its contents with an exhaled gasp.

'What on earth do you want? I have nothing of real value here.' He stammered.

'That's not what I'm here for, Doc.' She smiled and pushed another of her business cards over the table, her gun holding steady, pointing directly at MacFarlane's core. At all times she remained out of reach preventing him from even thinking about trying any stupid heroics.

'And before the grog gives you any Dutch courage don't let the size of my little friend here fool you. She's a Glock .45 Auto compact semi-automatic pistol and while she only carries six rounds each slug has a muzzle velocity of around 957 feet per second. I'm sure that I don't need to tell you what kind of damage that would do to you at this range, Doc.' Becca slowly crossed her legs and eased back in her chair placing the gun in her lap. The good doctor relieved, but only slightly, not to be staring directly down the barrel of a gun.

'This says you're a journalist,' the doctor blurted in incredulity, 'Flo did mention your visit earlier this evening.' He paused. 'But you're no journalist really are you?

'Well I have my moments, but no that's not the day job really.' She raised her eyebrows giving him an open expression, then said, 'I'm going to put the gun away now, George, do you mind if I call you George? But I want you to remember that my organisation take what we are going to talk about very seriously and we won't hesitate to deal with any loose ends should they become troublesome, do you understand me?'

'Yes, yes of course, anything.' He nodded furiously.

'Ok just sit back and relax, George nothing is going to happen but I need you to listen.' She paused to let him absorb what she was saying and to help put him at ease.

'I want to know more about the John Doe that you picked up yesterday on the beach at St Cyrus? It wouldn't normally have hit my radar but something was mentioned to the media about a distinctive scar on the back of the upper leg. What kind of scar was it?'

Looking at the business card Macfarlane gathered himself.

'Well, Becca, it was clearly a manmade scar which appeared to have be cauterised into the rear thigh on the right hand side, if I was guessing I would say that they had been branded.'

'That's what I had feared, so could you make out what the branding was an impression of?' She quizzed.'

'Not to start off with but we were able to lift an imprint off of the area and were able to take a look in more detail. I'm not trying to be funny or anything but it looked like one of those smiley faces you see on emails.

Becca puffed her cheeks out and exhaled a long stream of air.

'I take it that probably doesn't come as a complete surprise to you,' MacFarlane exclaimed, 'so do you mind if I ask you a question now?'

'Go on!'

'Well you mention that you are part of an organisation and clearly whatever happened at the beach yesterday is tied in with you sitting here in my living room and frankly ... you know what, can I have another one of those?' He seemed to run out of steam and pointed at the whisky.

'Here let me help you,' Becca offered, 'I think I might join you, too.' She warmed to him a little, yes he was an officious, middle aged, middle class wind bag, but she couldn't help but feel he was a straight up guy and would comply with her completely.

'Yes you're right, I do represent an organisation and we've been tracking a number of rising trends in criminality over recent years. Many of the types of crime that have been increasing alarmingly we tend to leave to other Governmental agencies who've been charged with dealing with such matters. However, I guess you could say that we have the luxury of working outside of official circles and have been paying particular attention to the rise in human trafficking which is becoming nothing short of a global industry.' She paused. 'George what these gangs are doing would make you sick to the core – they're predators and it's our job to deal with the very worst of them.'

'But I'm curious,' he ventured, 'if I've got it right you work for one of the law enforcement agencies – so why didn't you approach the ACC directly? I'm sure the police would be more than happy to cooperate.'

'Let's just put it this way, George, apart from the force being a leaky sieve, I think that there could be some resistance to my methods – but don't look so worried I can assure you we really are the good guys here.' She swigged the whisky pausing for a moment to fully enjoy the sensation.

'You're right of course, George, the body washed up on the beach yesterday would appear to have been a victim of the particular gang we're on to. And the smiley is their trade mark often branded, sometimes tattooed, onto their property as they like to think of these poor souls. I reckon your John Doe was either in transit from Rotterdam to a drop off, probably one of the many harbours up the north east coast, or had already been sold on to some unscrupulous operator with vessels in the North Sea – something obviously went wrong, perhaps he made a bid for freedom and ended up going overboard. But what this does tell us is that this area in the north east is certainly gaining significance in this grizzly trade.'

MacFarlane fidgeted in his seat.

'So why the cloak and dagger stuff here, what is it that you need from me?'

'Well if I'm right George, then I'm figuring that you will have also discovered something else of interest on the victim. Perhaps something that you are keeping back from the public.

'How did you know? He blurted, we were under strict instructions directly from the ACC to keep that out of the public's eye.

Reaching into her jacket pocket Becca pulled out a plastic evidence bag containing a small black object about two centimetres square.

'Here's one I prepared earlier. I'm guessing it's identical to the one that you found on the body, right?'

'Right.' He agreed, 'it was actually under the skin directly beneath the mark.'

'It's a long ranged Radio Frequency Identification chip – or an RFID for short. A bit like some of the tracking technology that product manufacturers use to track goods around the globe. These little suckers are particularly high tech in that they appear to have super encrypted data meaning that our guys are struggling to get much of a handle on who its talking to but it is a little marvel as it appears to use pretty much any communication network to signal its whereabouts, wifi, mobile networks, various radio band and a bunch of other stuff that sounded like it came straight out of NASA.'

MacFarlane was stunned.

'One problem is that they automatically shut down after a certain timeframe. An inbuilt fail safe against detection you might say. So whatever we do we have to do it quickly.'

'So how do I fit in to all of this?'

'It's very simple George, I want you to swipe the chip that you extracted from the John Doe and give it to me. This one is a dummy that one of our lab coats mocked up for me – just leave this one in place of the original.'

'I couldn't possibly do that,' he said pouring another whiskey stepping over to the sofa and slumping down. He rested his head against the back of the sofa running his hands through his thinning grey hair. 'I mean that would be illegal,

I'll ... I'll be in all kinds of trouble if they find I've tampered with evidence – and besides, sounds like you guys ought to just be able to wade in and take things over anyway.' He stammered again.

'George, listen to me and listen good – you won't get into any trouble and nobody will know that the chip has been switched. The dummy looks just like the real thing and has been specially designed to such a high spec that only the bad guys will know it's a fake using the right equipment. As for you getting into trouble – well you know what, George, just imagine the trouble you'll be in if you don't do this.' Becca patted her holstered pistol under her left arm.

She told George where she was staying and agreed that he would drop the chip off the next day.

Walking down Kirk Brae the weather had settled. She felt the static in the air, at least there was something that was making the hair on the back of her neck stand on end. As she stepped out of the glow of the street lamp she swivelled rapidly, hand on the stock of her gun ready to draw.

I must be getting jumpy in my old age, she mocked herself. She unlocked the door of her hire car. After getting in she put it into gear and carefully pulled away.

Easing back onto the North Deeside Road she glanced at the camera on the passenger seat.

'Right now for a spot of wildlife photography!'

# Nine

As soon as he had walked through the door of the apartment Floyd could feel the friction in the air. Yvette was home he could tell that much from the note pad on the dresser and the fact that the burglar alarm had been disabled.

'Hey, Yvie, I'm home – and just to prove it here I am.' He endeavoured to relieve the tension.

He wandered through the hallway and into the living room expecting to see her there, but no sign of her. He then realised that she was through in the bedroom and could make out that she was talking on the telephone. With the bedroom door only ajar try as he might he was unable to fully make out what she was saying; only the occasional word was audible.

'Ok I'll pick you up at ten from the airport. Better go, I think that's him back ...'

Floyd quickly and nimbly took a few large steps, retracing himself back towards the entry hall. After all he would hate for Yvette to think he was snooping on a private conversation. But nevertheless it all felt wrong. Apart from what he could make out from her side of that muffled conversation there was something else that felt out of place, he just couldn't put his finger on it.

He quickly scanned the room, he only had a moment. What was it?

There, that's it, in an apartment where everything had its place he quickly spotted his laptop perched on the kitchen worktop. It was difficult to see at this angle but, yes plugged into the side through the USB port was Yvie's iPhone.

'Floyd,' she announced pacing briskly from the bedroom, her face changing as if by the flick of a switch beaming at him with her million dollar smile, 'sweetheart you're home, I was beginning to wonder where you had gotten to.' Immediately distracting him.

She looped her arm around Floyd's waist embracing him and at the same time gently ushering him towards the bedroom.

'Why don't you get out of your suit, hon? I've just ordered in a takeaway. It shouldn't be more than a couple of minutes, and I think I've got a nice bottle of something I can open while you freshen up.' Running her hand across his chest he was once again totally compliant to her will.

What a day, he mused. Feeling totally unequipped to deal with so many strange occurrences, Floyd just sat there digesting the events of the last few days. He had become an accountant precisely because he liked the predictable, the sense of order in his life. But now, well, he didn't know what to think.

Having taken his time to slow his thoughts and change into his old cargo pants, oversized brilliant white beach shirt and flip flops, Floyd tidied away his work clothes, the ritual soothing his nerves. Slipping his own iPhone into his cargo pants a thought occurred to him. Lifting the bedroom phone out of its cradle he dialled 1471. The mechanised woman's voice informed him that the previous caller had withheld their number. Dead end.

Approaching him as he made his way back into the living area Yvette held two glasses of red wine. She proffered one to Floyd.

'Thanks, what've you ordered?' he asked. Glancing around the kitchen he noticed the absence of his computer. Trying not to appear too obvious he chose a CD from the rack

'Debussy's Clair de lune, I think,' he said more to himself than to Yvette. Then he moved around the coffee table and sat in his usual spot. Yes, there it was underneath the table exactly as he had left it earlier that day.

'Say Yvie, was that you on the phone just now?

'No,' she snapped, 'why do you ask? Pausing again, he sensed her mind racing. She continued, 'Oh when you just came in you mean? That eh, that was just me calling the takeaway – the usual curry – I hope that's ok with you, hon.' Standing up from the sofa she started busying herself with something in her handbag.

'That's sounds fantastic, I could murder a Balti. Actually I was wondering if Mum had called. She left a couple of messages earlier today.

'Did she, is there a problem?' Yvette enquired now alert.

'No, just some reunion that she's going to at the old school she used to work at. She'll be there this weekend, think she didn't want me to worry if I called her and missed her.'

'You never speak much about you mother, Floyd, you know it's probably about time you introduced me to her. After all we've been together a while now.'

'I will, Yvie, bear with me, she can just be a bit funny sometimes I know how her mind works – you know with us hooking up and living together so quickly.' Which wasn't untrue, if the whole truth were told, however, he thought she would judge Yvette too good for Floyd, not in a mean and spiteful way, but she would probably be painfully insightful leaving Floyd in no doubt that it would all end in tears. Better to hold on to the dream for as long as he could. But the problem was that Yvie was dead set on meeting his Mum, which, frankly, he thought a bit odd.

It was just after nine by the time they finished the takeaway and he could see that Yvette was getting fidgety, clicking away at emails on her smart phone.

'Look, hon, I've got to head off back to the hotel tonight we've just found out about the accountants who're coming in shortly to do a stock take, and well, it's just a headache that I can do without.'

'Babe, what's going on?' Floyd asked.

'Please, just don't.' She said, firmly raising her hand. She grabbed her phone and bag and raced away avoiding any further conversation.

He had hardly touched his wine yet. So, lifting the glass, he took three long drafts emptying it completely. 'What the hell is going on?'

He reached under the coffee table and pulled out his lap top computer switching it on. Normally it would take several minutes for the machine to whir through its start up routine since Floyd was in the habit of fully closing down his computer whenever he had finished with it. This time however, it opened onto his desktop in seconds as if it had been shut down in sleep mode, as if, he thought, somebody just closed the lid in a hurry.

Scanning the screen he noticed at the bottom that his email program was still open. He clicked on the icon to view his outlook account. What had she been looking for? Scrolling further down the folders he could see the folder that had been opened. It was headed *Mum*.

'What the hell are you playing at?' Floyd closed down the computer carefully. What he hadn't noticed though was that if he had looked closely at the system tray he would have seen that both the firewall and protection software to his computer had been disabled.

Pouring himself another glass he recalled the earlier conversation with Duggie about finding out where the email had been sent from earlier in the day. Why were all of these things happening to him, and why now?

Scrolling through his contacts he punched Duggie's name on his phone. It rang.

Duggie picked it up almost straight away. 'Hey, Floyd, I was just thinking about you. I've just run that IP address diagnostic and it seems that the originating server is in Swindon. As to where the sender was when the email was despatched could be anywhere within a twenty mile radius to be honest. Look can't stop to chat catch you tomorrow.'

'Thanks Duggie I owe you.'

'Big time!' Duggie hung up.


He must have fallen asleep on the sofa as the clock on the wall told him it was past one in the morning. Still no sign of Yvette.

As he gathered his wits about him a thought occurred. He felt guilty for feeling suspicious but you had to admit that Yvette had changed and something was going on. As he imagined his mother's words of caution, the worm of jealousy started gnawing away in his stomach convincing him that she was cheating on him, after all that would explained so much right? He sat up quickly and grabbed his phone. He had an idea.

Opening up the iPhone again he clicked through the general settings and opened the 'Where's my iPhone' setting. When Floyd won the phone Yvie set him up on her account. This meant they could buy music and Apps on the same account. It also occurred to Floyd that it meant they could track each other's phones with that handy little App you can use if you lose your phone.

The screen filled with a map of the UK and a flashing blue dot covering Aberdeen. As the system calibrated the dot shrunk and zoomed in to indicate exactly where Yvette's phone was. Only half expecting it to be over the hotel near Market street where she was supposed to be, Floyd's heart sank when the blue dot homed in to a location about seven miles from where she said she would be, confirming, he thought, his worst suspicions.

What could he trust, he felt as if his life was just one big deception and he was the mug. 'Bet she's having a big laugh right now at my expense.' He spat out in his rage and humiliation, the worm digging deeper – doing its worst.

'Fuck it,' to hell with her. He didn't know what his plan was and in fact it was all a bit of a blur. Perhaps he'd had too much red wine too quickly. But before he knew it he had packed his travel bag, grabbed his laptop and loaded them into the back of his car. They were chalk and cheese him and Yvette, he was seeing that now. I mean, he thought, look at your car a Y reg VW Polo, cost you five hundred pounds, she drives a new Audi TT sport. 'Who do you think you're kidding, you're a loser, Floyd.' Getting in the car he drove. After a few minutes driving randomly towards the outskirts of the city he realised he knew exactly where he was heading.

# Ten

The farmhouse was situated at the end of a rough narrow track itself leading to a small road about seven miles south west of Aberdeen. The area was sparsely populated, the occasional steading and a few more modern buildings inhabited by well-to-do oil workers, but no direct neighbours for almost a mile. It was the perfect hideout.

From the outside you would be excused for thinking the place was deserted, with an air of dereliction the odd decaying piece of agricultural equipment from the fifties and sixties rusting away in the undergrowth.

He pulled the VW Polo into a lay-by shrouded in complete darkness by an overhanging tree. Completely hidden despite the brightness of a full moon.

This is it, he thought, this is where her phone is located.

As he stepped out of the car it was only then that he realised he had no coat. The clouds had passed by from earlier in the evening leaving a clear sky and the temperature was plummeting. With only his white beach shirt covering his arms Floyd shivered and hugged himself to stay warm. His need to know, to get answers, however drove him onwards picking up his pace as he jogged up the farm track.

As he approached the building he stooped behind the old bailing machine, gradually making his way around the back of the house. From there he could see the Dutch barn. Made of corrugated metal, like the bailer it too was corroded and discoloured by years of harsh weather. As his eyes became accustomed to the moonlight he could make out the new panels that had been added to the barn, completely sealing the structure making it weather proof. It also prevented prying eyes from seeing in too he thought.

He was beginning to think that he was on a wild goose chase when the throaty sound of an old Land Rover starting up broke the silence on the far side of the barn. As Floyd manoeuvred himself he caught a glimpse of a silhouette. He was a large man, bald-headed with a strong wiry frame. The man was lifting a large sack around a metre and a half in length straining to throw it over his shoulder. He walked to the Land Rover and heaved the bag into the back with a thud. Lifting the tailgate up, he secured the back of the vehicle.

Floyd made himself as small as possible certain that the man was staring directly at him. Unable to see his features he held his breadth frightened of giving himself away.

The man reached for an object in his army trousers, a lighter. He flicked the lid and lit the flame lifting it towards his face to light the cigarette that was in his mouth. In a second the light was extinguished. Stepping over to the idling Land Rover he looked behind him and over his shoulder towards the barn door.

'Why don't you have a little more fun with the merchandise *mymoj slatki izopačena stvar* , how you say – my sweet deviant.' Getting into the Land Rover he gunned the motor and pulled away in a cloud of choking diesel smoke. Watching the rear lights bouncing down the track Floyd trembled as the image of that face illuminated for just an instant burned into his retinas he wouldn't forget that face in a hurry.

His eyes turned in the direction of where the man was shouting to catch a glimpse of a figure turning back into the barn. The latch clanging shut.

Furtively glancing all around him Floyd half ran half walked across the yard to the side of the barn, working around the perimeter looking for a window or gap to see in. At last he located a panel of corrugated iron where the bolt and washer had fallen through. He bent down to peer in with his right eye closing his left, which helped a bit. There was a source of light inside and while his view was partially obscured by hay bales he could make out a rough functional table along the opposite wall. On the table he saw a computer next to what must be a mobile phone. Scanning along the surface of the table were a couple of kidney shaped stainless steel bowls and immediately in front of which were numerous surgical instruments neatly laid out on green paper towels.

She stepped immediately in front of his spy hole, so close in fact that she blocked his entire view of the inside of the barn. He gasped at the realisation that the woman must have been right behind the wall mere inches away from where he was crouching now.

As she walked towards the table he could progressively make out her outline, shrouded in a long overcoat she stepped towards the table and picked up the phone.

Was it her, was this his Yvie?

She rang the number, Floyd straining to hear. In the still night her words were as clear as a bell.

'Hi, hon, it's only me, Yvie, looks like I'm going to be tied up tonight with the night shift staff. If you pick this up before going to work can you wait in for me before setting off.' she was staring now at the screen on the computer punching the keys flicking through files until she seemed to find what she was looking for. 'In fact I'll send you a text, too, as I know you'll pick that up.'

She hung up.

'Shit,' he whispered through gritted teeth, fumbling through his pockets trying to locate his phone. Quickly he powered it off a second before she pressed send.


He stumbled back to his hiding place behind the bailer, sitting on the damp soil he held his hands over his face overwhelmed at what he has seen. He held both of his hands over his mouth to try and control his need to roar out with frustration, to kick in the door and confront her to make her tell him what was going on and … and what? That everything was OK, that she really did love him?

No, he knew that it wasn't going to be OK but he did deserve answers and he was going to get them. He was going to get them now god dammit.

Standing up he began to march back around the barn his resolve getting firmer with every step.

Stepping around the north side, the barn cast an inky black shadow across his pathway back to the spy hole. Without any sound a figure stepped out immediately behind Floyd tightly clasping a hand around him and over his mouth while simultaneously pressing a pistol painfully against his right temple.

'Get back to your car you damn fool.'

# Eleven

Driving back towards the South Deeside road at a speed much too fast for the VW Polo Floyd gripped the wheel tightly. The whites on his knuckles giving away his tension.

'Shit, Becca, no really, what the hell are you doing here? This is just getting so unreal.'

'Look, Floyd just calm down or you'll kill the both of us, I don't think this car was made for speeds over forty miles an hour. So do us a favour and slow down.' She paused – she had seen people like this dozens of times, she knew that the axis of his world had just tilted. He needed to let the adrenaline subside.

'There will be time for questions later, but let's just get you to a safe place first, you can't go home. I'm staying at the Station hotel so let's go to the multi-story car park at Union Square and dump your car there, you'll have to stay with me.'

'Why would I need a safe place, what are you talking about?' His voice now a high staccato.

'Just drive.' She pulled out a small hip flask took a swig of the Malt within and offered it to Floyd. He wrinkled his nose then thinking again grabbed it and gulped the burning liquid. Coughing and spluttering he handed it back.

'You just better hope I don't get stopped by the police now.' He said.

Pulling out her pistol she said, 'for their sake they had better not pull us over !'

'What the hell is going on?' He said and he began to weep.


Becca pushed the key card home into the slot of the door to her room. She held the door open for Floyd who appeared to be showing the signs of shock. She hurried him in.

'Well this is it.' She grabbed the bottle of Southern Comfort off the shelf and both tumblers in a single hand. 'I know you've had a helluva day and you've probably got a million questions, not least what am I doing here? Here have this, it'll help.'

He took the drink and stared at her hardly believing his eyes that it was his Becca sat there on the bed in front of him. Only it wasn't really the same Becca. Thirteen years had passed and she was different in just about every way. Before she was a young person with red hair, a warm complexion, freckles. She always had a great figure but had something of the girl next door about her, too – his best friend. Today, yes she was the same person but hard and dark. Not just to look at with jet black hair, deep mascara and make up, but inside, too, there was an intensity about her, an insatiable energy.

'So let's do this, Floyd, I want you to tell me everything that has been going on over the last few months, then I'll tell you everything that I can tell you.

So he did, Becca sat silently for most of the next hour and a half as Floyd updated her on what he had been doing, his work, his life in Aberdeen, how he had met Yvette, their whirlwind romance and moving in together. Then he went on to explain the strange events over the last few days leading to that evening. She avoided interrupting him as much as possible, skilfully interrogating him by building his confidence and teasing out every little minor detail.

'And that's when you stopped me dead in my tracks,' he said, 'one way or the other I was going to have it out with her.'

'I'm glad I saw you then, Floyd; I think if I hadn't then things would not have gone well for you. As I'm sure you are beginning to realise things are not what they seem.'

He reached over for the bottle. 'May I?'

'Be my guest, me, too, please.'

He poured. 'Well that's me, that's how I got into this state, it's funny really isn't it, you know until a couple of days ago, I thought my life was perfect. I was happy. But now I know it was all just a lie. Go on I've spilled my guts to you … now it's your turn, Beccs.'

'Alright. Fair's fair I suppose.'

'As far as most people are concerned I'm a freelance journalist and that's true, I am. I do a lot of my own camera work, too, hence that lot over there.' She pointed to the camera case.

'I know,' he said, 'I've read a number of your articles in the Sunday supplements.'

'Right, but that's not all I do, in fact it's not really what drives me. Ever since leaving Oxford I've also been involved with various security agencies of the British Government. I can't really say much more than that.

Floyd furrowed his brow. 'Hang on a minute, so you're trying to tell me that a government agent would shoot a policeman, cos it seemed to me that's what you were suggesting earlier on?'

'Floyd, there's something you need to understand, the agency that I work for now was set up by the UK Government, but it is completely off grid. My authority is unquestionable and if I decide to act in extreme prejudice I have an absolute mandate to do so.'

'What,' he scoffed, 'bit like 007, license to kill?'

'Yes, Floyd – exactly like that! And what's more it appears to me that you've stumbled directly into the locus of our mission.' She paused to gather her thoughts. 'But I must confess that it's not entirely coincidental that I'm up here developing this arm of the mission. You see we have been seeing spikes of activity developing for some time. From our liaison with Interpol we have been able to covertly track a consignment from Dubrovnik which has ended up here in Aberdeen, and until now we didn't realise how substantial an operation was being carried out here. Until today that is.'

Floyd stared trying to process what was being said.

'I specifically assumed this leg of the mission once I read the report and saw your involvement.'

'But why? He blurted.'

'You, you daft bastard, because of you. I wanted to be here to help you.'

'But I'd have thought there was some sort of protocol to prevent people like you having conflicts of interest. I mean, what would your boss have to say about this?'

'Well Floyd, it's like this – I am the boss, most of my employees call me Ma'am or Commander. Mind you for security purposes nobody at the Unit or in government knows my real name, other than the PM of course, so I guess you could say that he's my boss.' They laughed a little and the tension eased a bit.

'But let me tell you a little more about the case, Floyd, there are some things that you need to know.'

They spoke for at least another hour until the wee small hours when they finally both collapsed exhausted on the bed.

A few miles away back at the apartment Si slipped the key Yvette had given to him into the front door. He slid quietly into the apartment a silenced Beretta in hand searching out its next victim. Quickly he worked his way through all of the darkened rooms in the apartment by torch light – it was empty. The sense of being cheated causing tension to rise the desire to kill ever present.

Controlling the burning rage inside he turned his attentions to locating the computer. It was vital to find it she had said. There was something on there that she needed and he would find it under the coffee table. '*Sranje*.' no sign of it. Still not to worry they would soon be able to locate it using the spy software she had installed onto it earlier that day.

Si carefully replaced everything in the apartment and shut the door.

He stepped back out into the street heading for the car. The only person seeing him leave was the bag lady pushing her trolley along the Grove, but nobody ever sees the bag lady even if she saw them; they just cross the road.

# Twelve

Back in the eighties and nineties, Floyd's mother worked in the back office at the school in Marlborough where Floyd studied throughout his teenage years all the way through to the upper sixth. She worked there part time – mostly to keep her sane; Doreen was an intelligent woman needing stimulation and in those early years she loved her job. In later years the work was increasingly vital to the household finances as Bobby's hours at the plant were reduced over and over despite union protests. Eventually Bob lost his job – Doreen's work keeping the whole family afloat.

As the local authority made further cut backs Doreen become responsible for scheduling classes for the lower school, too, which sometimes meant having to help the teaching staff with playground patrols – she didn't like doing these tasks, but needs must in those days. Doreen much preferred the office chat and became great friends with Doris, remaining the best of friends even to this day.

When the time came Doreen was happy to leave the school and move up north following Bob's reviving career after that event.

Even now when chatting with Doris on the phone when it gets mentioned it shakes Doreen to the core and she would always try to move the topic of conversation on to much nicer things. You see Doreen is one of life's optimists looking to see the positive in everything and the best in everyone. She also used to believe that all children were little angels sent from God – his gift to the world you might say.

And to all the world Tanya Gleeson looked just like a little angel: She was not. An intelligent and beautiful little girl Tanya became accustomed to getting her own way, by the age of seven skilled in the art of manipulation her personality became increasingly dark and sensation seeking. An arrogant child Tanya lacked empathy for any other human being, but a skilled actress she was able to hide a deep character defect from her parents, teachers and others in authority.

It was only a matter of time and that time of reckoning was June 1990 when the PTA at the junior school organised a summer term outing for all the primary three and four pupils. A trip to the glorious south coast, exploring Corfe Castle and then onwards to the beach near Swanage. It was a bright sunny summer's day and spirits were high. Doreen and Doris had been drafted in as extra responsible adults to look after the sizeable group of seven and eight year old kids.

It was during the melee of lunchtime when Doreen and one of the teaching staff carried out a headcount identifying that a couple of the kids must have wandered off. After a quick search they found them further up the hill standing close to a cliff edge deep in conversation – the sea and rocks some thirty feet below.

It was a very still day and the sea calm. And as Doreen and the teacher approached, Doreen implored the children to step back from the edge.

'We won't be long, Mrs Carter,' Tanya called sweetly over her shoulder, 'I was just telling Dean to stop coughing. He was doing it all the way down on the bus and it has been giving me a headache.'

'Children come away from there.'

'I told him,' she continued,' that if he didn't stop doing it then I would push him over the edge. That would stop him wouldn't it, Mrs Carter?'

'Oh do shuttup, Tanya, I can't help it I've got a tickly throat.' He spluttered while trying to unwrap a Fruit Salad sweet.

'Well then, you can't come back.' And with a sharp two handed shove Tanya pushed the shocked Dean over the edge. He hardly had time to scream during his descent onto the harsh unforgiving rocks below.

Turning around and walking towards the teacher and Doreen, Tanya gazed up at them beaming with her most angelic smile.

'I did tell him but he didn't do as I told him – so it's all his fault don't you agree, Mrs Carter?'


Following the death of eight year old Dean, the press had a field day; nothing had been seen like it before and many of the members of the inquest found it hard to believe a young girl of seven was capable of such a cold-blooded act. It was Doreen's and the teacher's testimonies that convinced the court of how that day's events actually unfolded.

Years of psychiatric evaluation and therapy followed for Tanya. Her family dutifully stood by her seeking review after review of her case, petitioning the judiciary, the probation service and local MPs. Eventually, now in her twenties, after passing through the hands of countless case workers and health care professionals it was clear that Tanya had responded well to her psychiatric therapy. When the time came around for the sitting of the Review Board all were in agreement that Tanya was now a stable young adult demonstrating an ability to modify her behaviour and able to successfully assimilate back into normal society. Formal applications were successfully made to the Home Office seeking her release on a lifelong licence and to be given a new identity – In early 2008 Tanya Gleeson became Yvette Semple and was a free woman after eighteen years of incarceration.

Yvette's parents tragically died in a boating accident six months following her release.

# Thirteen

Floyd Carter had been living a lie and as the light drifted into the hotel room the facts from his conversation the night before with Becca were slowly coming back to him. He remembered that after everything he had learned he felt angry – at being deceived by Yvette, but in God's name why? It just didn't make sense.

Propping himself up on his elbows he scanned the room expecting to see Becca when the telephone rang on the side table. Cautiously he lifted the receiver placing it to his ear.

'Hello.'

'Floyd, it's me Becca, I thought I'd let you sleep – you had a lot to process last night.'

He turned to the clock on the bedside table.

'Bloody hell, one o'clock, how on earth did I sleep so long? Why didn't you wake me?' He panicked, 'I'll be in so much trouble at work.'

'Easy, tiger, just take a few deep breaths. After all we did give that bottle a bit of a scare last night, don't know about you, but I felt decidedly ropey this morning. I hope you'll forgive me but I also slipped you a mild sedative.'

'You did what?'

'I thought you needed it. Look, I've had a few errands to run anyway, which have been quite illuminating – would you like to get together and grab a bite to eat. I'd like to update you on what I've found – you up for that? Oh, and don't worry about work I've pulled a few strings to smooth that out for you – very accommodating your Managing Partner when you say the right things.'

'What have you done, Becca?' His voice rising a tone in alarm. 'You know what, I don't think I really want to know right now.' He flopped back onto the bed all the fight draining out of him.

'But I will take you up on your offer for lunch, just let me freshen up. Where do you wanna meet?'

'I'm just down Waterloo Quays at the moment so why don't I grab a table at Frankie and Benny's in Union Square. See you there at one thirty.

'It's a date.'


The waiter led him to her table offering them menus to choose their meals from.

'No need,' Becca said, placing her order there and then going on to order for Floyd as well.

'Wow,' he said, 'that's exactly what I would have ordered.'

'Cheers.' They raised their glasses of water.

Sitting in silence neither knew exactly what to say. But it was Becca who broke the silence.

'Floyd, I want to level with you. When I came up here, as I explained last night, it was to track down and eliminate some of the key members of a particularly nasty gang involved in human trafficking. Their activities have become more brazen and appear to be expanding, and I might add increasingly savage in their approach. If I'm right we need to get back to that farmhouse to get a closer look at what's going on inside.'

'I don't get it,' he said while simultaneously tearing the label idly off of the water bottle, 'and do you know what really confuses me, well apart from everything of course, is that if Yvette works for this outfit then why is she so dedicated to her job at the hotel? I mean she spends God knows how long in that place always at the beck and call of her bosses in the Netherlands.'

'You do know that peeling the label off of a bottle is a sure sign of sexual frustration.' Becca teased him.

Quickly Floyd released the bottle brushing away the fragments of paper onto the floor.

'It's a good point, though, one that I've been giving some thought to as well.' She continued. 'Could be that we're looking at this gang's activities as simply part of a wider more organised group. You know, like some companies diversify into different industries all reporting to a group head.' She grabbed the neck of the bottle, twisted the lid and poured him and her more water.

'I reckon that … the Netherlands you say?' He nodded.

'This is probably where her bosses are – and I don't just think they will be hotel chain executives, probably more like crime syndicate members – the slave trade being only part of the business, probably try to cloak their activities with other ventures like hotels, casinos all sorts. I'll speak with my assets overseas see if we can start to join together a few more dots. Might be useful to gather some of the contact records such as emails, phone numbers that sort of thing.

'You're making it sound like some sort of Mafia organisation.'

'You know what … that's exactly what it sounds like. And the Mafia isn't just one outfit it's a term used increasingly for organised crime anywhere, you know like Russia, the Ukraine as well as the traditional Sicilian Cosa Nostra.'

'So hang on, you're telling me that Yvette works for this Mafia gang running one of their legitimate businesses and also involved with Human Trafficking. Seems a bit far-fetched doesn't it?' said Floyd, sitting back in his chair and giving a sigh. 'But I do have to admit that the one thing the past week has taught me is that there are a lot of things that seem far-fetched, but that doesn't stop them from being true.'

'Human trafficking is a wide church, we see this trade being used for all sorts of things. You know, like sexual slavery, forced labour and prostitution, and even ..,' as she was saying the words another thought entered her mind. 'Even for the harvesting of organs and surrogacy – shit, Floyd you said that you saw what you thought were surgical instruments in the Farmhouse didn't you – I'm getting a really bad feeling about this.'

Rising from her seat she threw a fifty pound note on the table.

'Grab your coat we've got work to do.'


Speeding down the ramp of the multi-story car park in the rental car Becca navigated her way out onto Market Street accelerating hard to beat the lights, narrowly missing a bus that had just pulled out from the bus station.

'So where are we going now?' Floyd asked grabbing the handle on the car door to prevent himself from slamming into the dashboard as she tore around the mini roundabout onto Riverside Drive. 'Shit, Becca, if they don't kill us first I think you might.'

'Back to the Farmhouse I think that might be where they're holding them, you know their captives. We've got to get in there. No time to waste.'

'Becca, just hang on a minute, couldn't this be dangerous – I mean they could have guards there, and that guy I saw last night, I'm sorry but he just looked plain evil. In fact the more I think about it I reckon it could have been a body that I saw him dumping into the back of his Land Rover.' After a moment's intake of breath, as Becca drove perilously around a couple of bends, the tyres of the car screeching in protest, he found his voice again.

'No! No, this is all wrong, Becca, we need to call the Police, let them deal with it.

'Can't do that, if we wait for them it could be too late. And besides, I met up with a guy from the Path' Lab this morning seems like all hell is breaking loose at Area Command Police Head Quarters. Looks like our boys in blue have discovered that some evidence has been tampered with in the John Doe case.'

He turned to face her – his own face pale from fear and bewilderment. 'Has that got something to do with all of this?' He questioned.

'Possibly,' she started, 'In fact probably I'd say it also means we can't trust anybody and we're on our own on this one. You're going to have to trust me, Floyd. Anyway, I've got my kit in the boot.'

'Your kit', he questioned, 'what do you mean your camera bag? You're hoping to gather evidence, is that the plan?' He mocked. 'And besides you left it all back in the hotel room.'

Becca patted his knee as if reassuring a nervous child. 'That's not the kit bag I was talking about.' She grinned, placing both hands back on the steering wheel. She shifted the car down a gear swinging left at the end of Leggart Terrace and gunned the engine ferociously. 'Five minutes, Floyd, hold tight!'

# Fourteen

It was only three in the afternoon when Floyd checked his watch. It was unbelievable to think that they were in this place not much more than twelve hours before and yet it seemed like a lifetime ago.

'What's the plan Becca?' He asked as they sailed past the entrance to the lane. There were fields on either side of the road that they were on and patches of woodland peppered the countryside.

'We can't just wander up to the front door, so we're going a little further along this road. I spotted a lay-by last night the other side of that hill. There's plenty of tree cover. So we'll park up there.'

She manoeuvred the car into the lay-by being careful to pull in behind a large evergreen bush. Safely hidden she popped open the boot of the car.

'What now?' Floyd demanded.

'Come on, out you get and I'll show you.'

Becca lifted the hatch on the boot at the back of the car revealing a large ridged suitcase. Her nimble fingers rapidly turned the numbers of the combination locks and then she flicked the latches sideways clicking it open. She lifted the lid of the case revealing a miniature arsenal of weapons.

'Holy Shit, Becca who are you – and what have you done with the Becca I knew?'

Smiling coyly she said, 'Still the same old tart, but I guess perhaps it just took me a while to show my true colours. Now then ...' She lifted a small machine pistol out of the foam protector, ramming home a magazine into the handle. 'I'll take the Uzi, and the Glock, here you take the Sig p238. You ever fired a gun before? She asked as she strapped on an ammo belt fully loaded with additional magazines.

Floyd looked down at the pistol that Becca had just thrust into his hand as if it were a dead animal. 'Never,' he declared, 'and honestly, I'm not sure that I could.' He confessed.

'Well let's hope it doesn't get to that.' She gave him a brief thirty second run through of the basics, safety, how to hold it and most importantly – shoot to kill, no messing. 'Come on follow me.' She instructed.

They followed another much rougher track that appeared to be used for vehicles carrying equipment to service the overhead power cables marching off into the distance. Keeping close to the wooded areas, Floyd was amazed at Becca's ability to work with the situation and make a plan on the hoof. She had always been very resourceful.

Working their way along the track they found a barbed wire fence about half a mile further around the edge of the woods. 'This looks like it should be the western boundary to the farm. Let's get as close as we can to get a good look. We can use the woods for cover, just keep your wits about you I doubt it but we have to assume they have prepared the groundwork, you know – early warning, perhaps even anti-personnel.' She was talking to herself now going through her own mental check-list in preparation.

'What the hell are you saying, Becca? D'you reckon there'll be booby traps around here...? Shit what the f ...' She slammed her hand back onto his mouth bringing him up short.

'Don't move,' she ordered. Her senses all alert.

'What is it?' Floyd asked, trying to keep the panic out of his voice, but failing miserably as Becca removed her hand.

'Look over there in the undergrowth,' she pointed, 'do you see that small metallic rectangular object? It was only about twenty metres away and at an angle to them making it difficult to see properly.

'Well,' she said, 'that's an M18A1 Claymore. If we got close enough you would see written on this side of the device, "front towards enemy." It has a kill zone of about a hundred metres and a sixty degree arc.'

Jabbing her finger she pointed the direction she wanted them to take encouraging him as she fought throught the bushes, 'don't worry this is a walk in the park just do what I do and keep your eyes open.'

They weaved their way around the Claymore, taking good care to watch out for other hazards. Fortunately there weren't any. Eventually they broke out into an opening behind the wood store on the far side of the barn that Floyd had been sneaking around last night. The coast was clear, no sign of anyone.

'Are you OK Floyd,' she turned to look at him as they squatted behind the wood store, 'you're looking a bit green around the gills there.'

'Sorry, Beccs, it's just … oh forget it, just give me a moment to control my nerves.'

'Here, take this,' she passed him a small capsule, 'sorry don't have any water, just pucker up and swallow.'

'What is it?'

'Just something that sometimes helps my agents when they're out in the field. It's a synthetic drug, acts a bit like beta blockers and a dash of Prozac. All low level stuff but it helps deal with the anxiety without disrupting motor function and judgement.'

'Is it legal?' He asked knocking his head back swallowing the tablets.

'If I say it is – then it is! Now, are you ready?'

'There's nobody here,' she said to herself as they entered into the barn, 'it's like the Marie Celeste.

They explored the empty space of the barn as rapidly as possible in search of any clues that it might give up.

'Over here, Becca, help me get this hatch up, looks like there might be a cellar or something under the floor.' Floyd strained at a metal hatch at the rear of the barn. Everything else in the barn looked as you might expect it to. If anything it was perhaps a little too neat and tidy – giving nothing away.

Together they forced the latch and lifted the lid up easily on its well-oiled hinges. From there all that could be seen was a worn set of wooden steps sinking down into the darkness.

'Right, you stay here, Floyd, I'm going in.' Extracting a torch from somewhere on her person Becca confidently descended down into the cellar, a thin beam of light flicking this way and that as she gave her eyes time to adjust.

Floyd immediately felt alone and vulnerable with Becca out of sight. Wanting to be useful he paced over to the entrance of the barn taking up position just inside so that he could peer out from time to time looking out for any unexpected and unwelcome visitors. It occurred to him that it might be a sensible precaution to get his gun out and have it at the ready. Better keep the safety on though, he thought.

With Floyd deep in concentration Becca had to call to him a number of times to attract his attention. 'Floyd get down here, I want you to see something.'

He carefully put the Sig back into his shoulder holster and jogged back across the barn to climb down the steps into the gloom, following Becca's voice.

Becca had changed the settings on her torch. It was now illuminating a neon tube in the handle. And while this had a much less intense light than the point setting it was able to cast a dim glow over most of the cellar.

'What am I looking at, Becca? He asked. 'Just looks like a load of old junk to me, bit like my Dad's garden shed.' He flapped his hands in front of his face feeling the cobwebs and dust settling onto him making him uncomfortable.

'Here, look behind these folded shipping boxes.'

It took Floyd a few seconds to realise what he was looking at, his hand went up to his gaping mouth. As he peered around the stacked boxes and with his eyes adjusting to the gloom, too, he shuddered at the sight in front of him. 'Oh shit, Beccs, are they what I think they are – and what I think they're used for?' All the way along the back wall of the cellar, which he now realised was considerably longer than had appeared on first impressions, were an assortment of wire cages – much the same as you might expect to see in a dogs' home or a laboratory – each about five feet deep by three wide and three high. As Becca stepped in closer to look she saw that most of the cages still contained paper thin mattresses which were heavily soiled by their previous occupants. All, however, were now empty, their doors swinging wide open.

As they looked around them they counted six cages along which were then stacked three high. Eighteen in total. There were still fragments of hair, blood stains and other traces still visible even in the dimming light from Becca's torch, which was now beginning to fade fast. Probably where the captives frantically tried to break out of their confines, she thought.

'Don't touch anything Floyd,' she instructed, 'I'm going to call in a flash forensic squad from Athena Central to work the grid here. We'll also instruct the Home Secretary to make certain the lid is kept shut on this; we don't want the local boys in blue getting involved here, at least not yet.'

Her back was turned away from Floyd who was glancing around under a trestle table adjacent to the stack of cages. 'Over here, Beccs, it looks like there's something down here. It's nearly slipped all the way through the floor boards. Let me see if I can get hold of it.' He tried snagging the corner with his fingernails several times worried that he'd push it all the way through. But after a couple of goes of trying he managed to get purchase on the corner, then gently pulled being careful not to tear it. He passed it to Becca who still had the torch, while he got back up onto his feet.

'Well, Floyd,' she said staring at what turned out to be a photograph, 'I guess this puts it beyond all doubt that it was Yvette who was here.'

He held the photograph at an angle trying to get a better look as Becca held the light steady for him to help see the image more clearly. It was one he recognised immediately and was very familiar to him. In fact it was the same as the picture that was framed and hung on his living room wall. The photograph was taken about a year and a half ago of him and his mother smiling happily into the camera at a family wedding they were invited to somewhere in the West Country.

'What do you think this means, Beccs?' Floyd asked, but he knew in his heart that it was something that he should be deeply concerned about. After all, having a picture of your girlfriend or boyfriend on your desk at work is one thing, but a misplaced picture in a makeshift dungeon used for the modern day slave trade?

'Only one reason that I can think of Floyd.' She said.

'W—hat's that?'

'Well let's put it this way, it seems to me that Yvette knows you've sussed something out and probably wants to tie up all of the loose ends.'

'And I'm a loose end I suppose?' He fretted.

'Look, I'm not going to let that happen alright ... give me that; she snatched the picture out of his hand and slid it into some unseen pocket. Now let's just keep focussed and take as many pictures as we can of the scene without moving anything, then let's get the hell out of here. I want to call this in within five minutes tops !'

Becca started snapping images on her Smartphone, starting at the back end of the cellar and systematically working towards the exit. Floyd had to switch his own phone on which took a few moments, but then he started to do likewise. A minute or two passed then Becca asked Floyd to go up top in order to keep look out again while she finished up.

He was happy to comply with Becca's request and as he hurriedly ascended the steps it was a relief to get back out of the gloom, his eyes adjusted to the light of an unusually bright day in the Aberdeenshire countryside.

As Floyd emerged from the hatch partially hidden by the metal lid the movement of a solitary figure stepping through the doorway to the barn registered in his peripheral vision. With the brilliant sunshine pouring in behind the figure it was impossible to make out who it was. Could it simply be a local was his first thought?

The muzzle flash that appeared in front of the figure was accompanied by the spitting sound of silenced gun fire aimed directly towards Floyd.

The bullet struck the top ridge of the metal lid that Floyd was holding open and standing behind ricocheting up into the rafters. Not waiting for a second shot to find its mark Floyd dropped immediately behind the door.

'Beccs, oh shit … he's got a gun, he's trying to kill me,' he blustered, stumbling backwards taking a couple of steps back down into the dark cellar, panic beginning to overwhelm him. Eventually Floyd managed to regain some self-control and pulled the Sig out of its holster and pointed it around the edge of the metal hatch. Pulling the trigger he braced himself for the noise and the recoil, but then – nothing happened. 'Oh hell, the safety you idiot.' He said to himself as he heard the footsteps of the assassin striding purposefully towards him taking shots at the metal door with every step forward, the bullets clanging viciously on the steel hatch. There was no way out, this was it – of that Floyd was certain. He braced himself for the inevitable when suddenly from beneath him Becca let rip with the Uzi which roared its terrifying blast tearing savagely through the floorboards and shredding their would be killer with over a hundred rounds in under ten seconds, leaving only a decimated corpse and a hideous mass of blood, splinters and bone fragments.

He looked at her aghast as she removed the spent magazine replacing it with a new one. 'Like I said Floyd, you stick with me I prefer your odds that way.' Stepping forward to him she caressed his cheek with her right hand, moving in to kiss him tenderly.

'Let's move out.'

# Fifteen

MacFarlane had been waiting in the lobby of the hotel for over half an hour. With every passing minute his anxiety was increasing, worried that somebody might recognise him. Lifting his half-moon glasses up onto his head against a rapidly receding hairline, he rubbed his eyes steepling his hands together in the process.

'George,' declared Becca as she and Floyd frogmarched into the hotel, 'sorry to have kept you waiting, we eh well I guess you could say we ran into a little trouble; nothing that we couldn't handle. But I'm ever so pleased that you are here. Perhaps we can talk somewhere a little more private – bar's open lets head in there.'

In the bar Becca carefully chose a booth well placed for its privacy away from any public areas. The three of them sat down.

'So I understand there has been a bit of a commotion with the duty sergeant in the evidence room?' Becca quizzed the pathologist in hushed tones.

'You could say that again. I submitted my report and your cloned chip into the evidence locker as you suggested first thing.' Later in the morning CID held a case briefing by which time it appears that a number of the investigating officers had reviewed the evidence.'

'You mean the encrypted chip?' Asked Floyd.

'Right,' replied George. 'Which strikes me as strange to say the least; I'd normally have expected it to have been despatched directly through to forensics to see what else they might be able to ascertain from the data on the chip.'

'Which of course we know is a dud right?' Retorted Becca. 'You have the real one with you here do you, George?'

'Yes, I have it here.' Reaching into his jacket pocket he was about to retrieve the chip, but Becca laid a hand gently on his elbow. The meaning obvious that he should wait as the waitress approached them to take their order; which they did carefully making sure nothing appeared unusual.

Having taken their orders the waitress spun around on her heels and walked away. George then slipped a small brown envelope containing the encryption chip over the surface of the table towards Becca.

'I've a team doing the clean-up job; they'll be getting into town shortly, they'll pick up the chip and get it over to our eggheads to see if they can crack it.' Becca told the other two. 'But the thing that interests me here is – why wasn't the evidence despatched immediately to forensics? My guess is that someone on the inside wanted to keep the chip where they could test it out with the right equipment, breaking the evidence seal was a smart way to hold it back and keep control of the evidence. It's like I said to you earlier this morning, Floyd, it seems these guys have got somebody on the inside.'

The three of them sat in virtual silence for a while each wrapped up in their own thoughts as the waitress brought their drinks over to the table.

'You know what, George, it might be time for you to take an impromptu vacation for a week or two – I'd recommend not leaving a contact number for your colleagues. I'll call you when you get back.' It was clear from her tone that it was an instruction rather than an idle suggestion and left MacFarlane in no doubt that it was in his best interests to comply. He sat there sipping his drink nodding his acknowledgement.

'I mean now, George … time for you to go.'

'Oh, I see,' he blushed, 'you mean right now.'

'Yup – and George,' she added, 'thanks.'

Getting up from the seat he stood there for a moment looking between them, unsure whether he should offer to shake hands. Instead he simply raised his right hand in acknowledgement. 'Bye then.'

Floyd turned to Becca still feeling somewhat euphoric, the chemical effects from the tablets she had given to him earlier maybe. 'So let me see if I've got this right,' he gushed, 'you somehow managed to enlist George MacFarlane, the Chief Pathologist, to tamper with evidence and switch that chip thing and replace it with a dummy?'

'Right, you're catching on quickly for a novice.'

'Incredible,' he said shaking his head at her brass, 'well I'm guessing that means you were expecting there to have been a chip like that on the body that they found and, what, you thought you would bring your chip along with the intention of flushing out anybody in the police who might be somehow attached to the gang?'

'Spot on, Floyd.' She mock punched him on the arm. 'You seem to have marshalled your thoughts since this morning.'

'Oh don't be too impressed, I think it's that upper that you gave to me earlier, it seems to have kept a lid on me – actually, you know what, after taking it all of that adrenaline in my system seems to flip from panic to a feeling of heightened excitement, I really felt in control for the first time in my life.'

Thinking back on the morning despite the danger they had encountered and the grim discovery in the barn, all Floyd could think about was the moment that Becca's hand gently brushed his cheek and that lingering tender kiss.

Their hands were both resting on the table top as they nursed their drinks. Floyd, moving his hand mere inches away from hers stretched his little finger the last inch until contact was made with her hand. Looking at her he admitted, 'Beccs in the last week my world has turned completely upside down; the love of my life turned out to be nothing of the sort, and there's a good chance that I'll have lost my job. And to cap it all I've even had to dodge anti-personnel mines and been shot at. But you know what,' he paused – 'at this moment, I couldn't be happier.'

'Now that does sound like the drugs talking.' They laughed companionably enjoying a few moments of light hearted conversation.

The waitress glanced at the nice young couple in the corner. It's great when the punters smile and laugh like that she thought. They always leave a bigger tip.


A bottle of Malbec later, it was becoming clear that the mixing of red wine together with military grade performance enhancing medication was a potent combination, and after the euphoria of that morning Becca led him to her room, undressed him and put him to bed. She knew that he would sleep for hours. Familiar with the effects of such medication she left him a large glass of water for hydration on the bedside table then leaned over his inert body ruffling his hair affectionately. A moment later she stood up straight and was all business again checking her pistol and equipment. She turned around purposefully, opened the door and silently shut it behind her as she left hotel room – she had a job to do running a sweep of his apartment, to see if any answers could be found there.

# Sixteen

Bristol Airport

'And how did our bit of business go in the Netherlands, Si?' Yvette asked as she greeted him at the arrivals point. Having arrived there less than an hour before herself, on the flight down from Aberdeen, she hadn't been able to speak with him before he had to switch his mobile telephone off upon boarding the aircraft at Schipol.

'Fine, like clockwork,' he grinned at her, his eyes dancing with a savage excitement. As they started heading towards the exit he said. 'I'll give you all of the gory details if you like, once we pick up the hire car.'

'I'd like nothing better, sweet cheeks,' she replied grabbing him playfully on the buttocks.

It was a small airport and so they only had to walk a short distance across the road to get to the Avis car hire booth. Once they were inside they didn't have to wait more than a couple of minutes to book their car, allowing them to get clear of the airport in good time.

The small blue Toyota Yaris sped confidently north towards the city of Bristol making swift progress. However, as they skirted around the southern fringes on the A4174 the daytime traffic got heavier and slowed them down.

'You know the traffic has always been a lot heavier down here than back in Aberdeen,' she said, 'I guess you'll have noticed that, too, especially in Camden.' He grunted in response to the inane small talk.

'I do still remember a lot of the places that we're driving through you know, just fragments of memories, images really but everything feels different here. All of the buildings seem to have different colours, the village pubs and greens it just feels like home.' She said nostalgically. 'And it was my home, until it was all taken away from me.' She could feel herself darkening in her mood and beginning to rant. She controlled her emotions; she still remembered how to use the techniques that had been taught in her anger management therapy sessions when she was inside.

'But listen to me talking all about myself. You said you'd tell me how it went in the Netherlands – as planned I hope?'

'Easier than expected, my dear,' the Croat replied. 'The good Mr De Groot had already taken the earlier flight from Edinburgh to Schipol so I didn't have to wait too long. Our paths crossed in the arrivals area before even getting into customs I myself having just flown in also. He made it too easy, I saw him stepping into the gents and followed him in. It took only a second to break his neck. It was empty in there so I was able to shove him into a cubicle and bolt the door shut. Easy yes! Not particularly elegant but it got the job done.'

'And did you lift his case? I should hate to have gone to that effort for the audit to still go ahead.'

Raising his hand he said, 'It's fine, all taken care of and once we're done down here we can get back up north to distribute the cargo, business as usual. You owe me one you know, having to move the cargo to the new lock up at short notice, took me all night – perhaps we should bring in some more help.'

'The fewer the better at the moment, it's early days yet so we won't always know who we can trust – I'll get soundings from our friend in the force. In the meantime I hope you left them with enough food and water for a few days.'

'Yes I did, don't worry – they'll need a hosing down when we get back but they'll survive, and the new lock up is perfect; they can make as much noise as they like. I also set up with live web feed directly to my phone, here look.' He turned the screen towards her revealing the luminous green image. 'So relax, enjoy the ride, you see, Yvette, sometimes you got to learn to be bit more like me and take pleasure in your profession. Once we get this monkey off your back we have good times. Yes?'

'Oh yes, Si, once I get this monkey sorted I am going to give you one helluva good time.'

# Seventeen

Early on the Saturday morning Floyd awakened to the sound of Becca drying her hair, the dryer droning through his subconscious mind bringing him around. He felt as if his limbs were made from lead but despite that he heaved himself up to sit upright in the bed as his hand sought out the glass of water to his side.

'I didn't think I had that much to drink – my mouth feels like a sandpit.' He exclaimed as he greedily drank the glass dry.

'You didn't,' Becca replied, 'it's just the side effects of those uppers I gave you. They don't usually have quite that effect, but I suppose together with the wine who knows. You did well by the way. Hope you're feeling refreshed now, you've been sleeping for over twelve hours.' She leaned towards the mirror pulling faces to assist in the application of that thick black mascara. As she did so her tee shirt started riding up to reveal a network of intricate tattoos.

'What do you think? She asked catching his reflection in the mirror.

'They're amazing, Becca, but I'm still trying to get my head around this new version of you. I know people change, but this whole bad ass thing you have going just seems the complete polar opposite from what you used to be.'

'Maybe,' she said, finishing her make-up. She spun around on the stool and fixed him with her stare.

'And perhaps maybe not,' she continued. 'You know a lot has happened since then but even then I knew that I needed something more. After my Dad died I guess I just fell into a slumber for a while. But you were there for me, Floyd, you know … you were on my wavelength. And ...' She hesitated.

'What, go on tell me.'

'Well, remember that night before you left Marlborough?'

'How can I forget, Becca, I'm embarrassed to say that was my first time, but I guess that was obvious.' Now laughing at himself.

'Yeah I figure that now, but it was mine, too, and frankly for me it was really special – because it was you.' Shifting in her seat she brushed away some invisible fleck off of her jeans. 'But it changed me, Floyd, when you left I had nobody. I mean I wasn't little Miss Popular you'll remember that, but honestly, I guess I felt abandoned.'

'I didn't choose to go, Beccs …' he started, then stopping realising that she needed to get this off her chest. 'I'm sorry.'

'I know … I know that now of course, but at the time I was heartbroken. I guess I developed an outer layer, a barrier against getting too close emotionally to people. Least that's what my counsellor tells me.'

'What, you're in therapy?' Guilt beginning to claw away on his insides.

'Well not really – just counselling sessions that I decided to take, you know this job can get a little intense sometimes – which I'm sure you'll have figured out by now. But I did start to find out more about my obsession with sex. You see since my university days I've had what you might call an over-developed sexual appetite, and my counsellor puts this down to me having emotionally fixated on you for such a long time and that has lead me to disassociate the emotional and the physical connection to all of my subsequent lovers.' Now it was her time to blush.

'Don't worry I didn't take advantage of you when I got you into bed yesterday, much as I was tempted to. You're quite something you know, I've never shown that kind of restraint for any other man I've taken to bed … or woman for that matter.'

Floyd was by now at a complete loss for words and gaped trying to form a sentence.

'Well, I don't know about you but I feel so much better for getting that off of my chest.' She said, turning back to the mirror she carried on touching up her make-up.

'There, right come on, you're not going to hang around in bed all day. Let's go get some breakfast.'

The same young waitress who looked after them last night was on the breakfast shift in the restaurant again this morning. 'Hello again, it's another glorious day out already; not often we get two in a row like this. She beamed.'

'Morning,' Floyd greeted her, as he sat on his own in the corner while Becca stepped outside to make some calls. 'I'll, have a coffee please?'

'Cappuccino right?' said the waitress jiggling on the spot.

'Right, how did you …' he ventured, confusion growing on his face.

'Last night, she said, 'I was serving your table last night. You and your girlfriend seemed to be having a great evening … were you celebrating something special?'

'Oh, she's not my … well we're old friends, we had a lot of catching up to do.'

The girl took his order before leaving him to his thoughts.

Becca wandered in moments later scanning the room and catching his eye. Her face lit up with a smile.

'All sorted?' He enquired. 'Have you been on the phone all this time?'

'Yeah, lots to do. Caught up with my local asset, too, updated me on the sweep at the farm house. Those guys are great, real professionals, they were all done by first thing this morning. They've also picked up the chip so it won't be long until we can get to work on cracking the code.

'Did they find anything useful at the farm house?' Floyd asked.

'You sound like you're getting into this kind of stuff.' She teased.

'I guess I am.' He said, and actually found he meant it.

'Well I guess that can't be the Dutch courage talking this time. You're quite something you know that, Mr Carter, and that's the second time today that I've told you that.' They laughed and enjoyed a few moments of small talk gathering their thoughts over the breakfast menu.

'Actually, though, the guys didn't find a whole lot else, sure there were quite a number of tissue samples that DNA can be extracted from, but those will mostly be the victims, I'm sure. So unless any DNA fingerprints are on a database somewhere in the world it's not going to help us much. Our best bet is still to crack the code on the chip, see where it leads us. With that information we'll then be able to hack into mobile and border agency networks and locate any poor souls in transit. But we won't have a window of opportunity for long though; once they smell a rat, they'll simply recode the encryption key, if they haven't already.'

It occurred to Floyd how open she was being. 'Beccs, much as I appreciate you taking me into your confidence, should I be hearing all of this?'

'I probably shouldn't be telling you, but if any of this gets out then of course I'll know exactly where the leak is.' She grinned at him, but with a glint of steel in her eye. 'And besides, I think this could be the start of something pretty special for both of us.' Her voice sunk an octave as she slid her hand along his brushing the hairs on his arm with her middle and index fingers. Goosebumps erupted all over his body at the thrill of her touch. Determined to keep his cool Floyd cleared his throat.

'So, where does this leave us?'

She sat back in the seat again, the atmosphere shifting in the booth once more as Becca refocused her attentions on the case.

'Well as far as I see it we have our plan so there's not a whole lot more that we can do at the moment to find the victims. What's more immediately worrying to me is what to do with you.'

Confusion slowly spread across Floyd's face. 'What do you mean?'

'I've been to your apartment while you were asleep, thought I'd take a chance to see if Yvette or any of her associates were there.'

'And ...?' He prompted.

'And nothing, well nearly nothing. The place looked just as you described it. Only one thing missing that I could see. The photo that you found at the barn of you and your mum. It wasn't there; just a picture hook on the living room wall where you said the picture was.'

'So what does this tell us?' Floyd asked in hushed, conspiratorial tones.

'Actually, probably quite a bit. So, firstly, there was no sign of forced entry, which tells us that it was either Yvette or somebody using her key to gain access. And secondly the photo was clearly important but I figure they must have been looking for something else, too, after all, Yvette knows what you look like and there will be dozens of pictures on Facebook since you set up your page if she wanted to target you for anything.'

'Whoa, whoa there, what do you mean target me?' Alarm was now creeping back into his voice. He took a moment, to recompose, reminding himself how impressed he thought

Becca had been with the new Floyd. Determined not to blow it he said, 'Sorry, Beccs carry on, perhaps we can get back to that.'

'Right, well so it occurs to me that they must have been looking for something else, and you know what, I reckon they were looking for your computer – I saw it in your bag yesterday when I was …' she paused smiling coyly. '… OK I admit it, I was snooping through your stuff – habits of a lifetime.'

'So you think there might be something …' Sitting back he slapped himself on his forehead, realising what it might be. 'Couple of days ago, Beccs, I received this bizarre email, I'll show you it as soon as we get back up to the room.'

He filled her in on the email and what he had been able to learn from Duggie. He touched his hand to his pocket, feeling for the photograph which was now dog eared in the pocket of his cargo pants.

'It's a crazy thought, Beccs, but are we missing the obvious here? He slipped the picture across the smooth table surface in front of Becca, tapping the faces looking up from the image.

'I'm not the only person in this picture, and unlike me mum is definitely not part of the Facebook generation. If somebody was targeting her, they'd need a photo right?'

Becca rummaged in her canvas shoulder bag retrieving a compact, moleskin-covered note book. Scribbling in the corner of a fresh page to get the pen working her excitement mounting in her voice she started dividing the page in three parts – the first she headed Aberdeen, the second Marlborough and the third, rest of the world. She scribbled a mind map across the page, joining captions with lines across the different sections.

'Look, Floyd, this is all about you <u>and</u> your mum,' she said, 'you said yourself that she was down in Marlborough again this weekend for a reunion and you also said that the IP address for that email is hosted on a server in Swindon – that's only half an hour's drive from Marlborough.' She jabbed at the page with her pen over-lining furiously seeming to reinforce her point.

'To be honest, Beccs, when you first showed up on the scene I thought it might have been you who sent the email. Between being shot at and high on Dutch Courage I guess I forgot to ask.'

'Well it wasn't me, haven't been back there in over a year. But it seems clear to me that we need to get down there as quick as we can, better give your Mother a call make sure everything's OK. Once we're finished up here let's double check on your computer and make sure there's nothing else there of interest. Meantime I'd better organise some transport.' She slipped her long fingers into a deep inside pocket to her leather jacket pulling out her phone.

'I'm not sure you'll have much luck getting a flight out today.' He looked sceptically at her.

'S'all right, thought we could catch a lift with the sweep up team, there's a Super Puma helicopter landing at the farm site at twelve noon. They can take us where we need to go, before taking the guys back to Central. C'mon, doesn't give us much time.'

# Eighteen

The morning had been one of those rare autumn occasions. Both of the elderly ladies had risen early in time for a leisurely breakfast and to watch the dawn gently unfold above the trees of Savernake Forest. The deep orange sunlight reaching out over the horizon gaining in its intensity giving way to a clear watery blue sky.

They had a lot to talk about enjoying the opportunity to reminisce, clucking excitedly about the fancy party that evening and wondering who was where and doing what. So engaged were they in their chatter that time seemed to slide by unnoticed.

'My goodness, Doreen, look at the time, poor little Henry will be crossing his legs if we don't take him out soon.'

Henry, Doris's pet pug, a little toy dog, was fussing around at their feet staring intently with the appearance of a grin turning up at his wrinkled muzzle. Happy to have another friendly human arriving the night before, Henry enjoyed Doreen's company, but was sure never to let Doris too far from his sight.

It was bright, but still cold and while the couple were adding on layers of clothing the telephone started to ring in the hallway. Doris and Henry shuffled off to answer the call leaving Doreen to her thoughts, happy to be back in Marlborough. This was the place where she had raised her children – happy days.

'Doreen,' Doris trilled, 'it's for you – young Floyd.' Walking back in the living room careful not to trip over Henry who was by now weaving in and around her legs with great anticipation, she handed the telephone over to Doreen.

'Hello, Floyd my dear.' There was an enquiring tone to her voice. 'It's nice to hear from you … is everything alright?'

'Hi, Mum, sort of, well …' He realised that he hadn't planned on what he was going to say to her. After all could he really tell her that he was the victim of an elaborate charade and that it was even possible that the perpetrators were somehow using him to get to her? It sounded incredible even to him … 'Yes sure, Mum, just wanted to check that you got to Doris's and that all's well?'

'Oh yes, Love, we've had a wonderful time catching up. In fact we were just about to step out of the door to stretch our legs and take Henry for a walk.'

'Henry?'

'Yes, Henry – Doris's Pug, dear little thing, she didn't have him when we lived here you see …' She trailed off.

'That's great, Mum, anyway, what I really wanted to tell you was that, well actually I'm on my way down to Wiltshire at the moment, too, and will be getting there soon – thought I'd look you up.'

'Well that will be lovely, Dear, why don't you pop in when you get here, I'm sure Doris will be thrilled to see you again – got to go, Floyd …'

'I will Mum, but I …' he ran out of steam realising he was talking to nothing. The phone was dead; it appeared his mother had already hung up.

# Nineteen

The darkness was absolute, a black velvet shroud enveloping Oksana and the others. How many she didn't know, none of them spoke much, each in their own hopeless spheres of existence, beyond shock, desperate foetal creatures. Time passed hour by hour, but the absence of light disoriented Oksana – the only indicators of time being the falling temperature and the gradual but steady escalation of agitation and distress of the inhabitants of that dark prison. When would he return, she both dreaded and craved the sound of the door opening – any minute now surely, please God. Her skin crawled with an increasing intensity – spiders parading over her skin, under her skin, the craving snagging at the base of her brain stem, piercing behind her eyes. Oh God how much longer?

Was it a day, two days, who knew how long she had been in this prison. She hadn't been in the last place long, maybe a week; the cellar of that barn. There were more of them there to start with. But her fellow inmates would be taken from there one or two at a time – she never knew what became of them. She couldn't always hear, but she did once make out the fragments of a conversation. In his deep Slavic accent she could hear the Man's words.

*'I take you now to your new Papa, he has paid very good price for you and has a very important job for you to do. And*

*don't forget you have the mark, so I always able to find you if your Papa tell me you run away – I look for you and I find you,'* his toned dropped as if confiding in someone, *'and when I find you – I hurt you, slowly. You will beg to die, but you will not die. Maybe I let you die in three days.'* His voice dark and malevolent.

*'Ah Mr Smith,'* the Man walked away, gravel crunching out of the barn and out of earshot – presumably Mr Smith was here to take possession of his goods.

And so it continued, their numbers depleting until there were only a handful. And last night, was it only last night? The woman was here too, she could hear their muffled tones, a rhythmical sound, but their conversation became increasingly frantic, clearly the woman was becoming alarmed by whatever it was they had to discuss. It was hopeless trying to make out anything other than snippets of conversation when the woman raised her voice.'

*'... I'm sure he suspects ... have to move site ... do it now ... I know where she will be ... kill Floyd ...'*


It had proven almost impossible for her to sleep chained and confined in those cages. Released once or twice a day for relieving and hosing down, she did however slide into some semblance of sleep in the very early hours of the morning.

A cool night, it was still and silent. Oksana awakened to a dim repetitive beeping sound. The sound slowly increasing in volume it was then accompanied by the crushing sound of gravel as an articulated lorry slowly reversed along the length of the farm track manoeuvring carefully until the rear doors were fully adjacent to the doors of the barn. As the driver turned off the ignition, the diesel engine gave a final rattle before stopping.

She followed the sounds of the footsteps above her head and over the wooden floorboards of the barn above. Somebody unlocked and lifted the hatch to the cellar; artificial light poured down the wooden steps and peered around the sides of the cardboard boxes.

There were two of them, one was the Man the other she had not seen before. He was big – bigger than the Man, but perhaps less intimidating, not taut and wiry, instead he was tall and stocky, and maybe a little older too.

One after another they released the remaining captives from their wire framed cells. Linen bags were pulled over their heads and their wrists were bound with plastic rip ties The procession of bedraggled human cargo was led to the upper barn along a wooden ramp and into the waiting trailer of the large articulated lorry.

The Man remained in the barn clearing the site while the larger man nervously ushered each captive into their new confines. The trailer of the lorry containing almost identical cages and loops for restraint as in the cellar of the barn.

The big man slammed closed the rear metal doors once the herd of broken humanity had been fully loaded into the trailer. Heaving hard he pulled home the lever sealing the freight container.

'Let's go,' Si instructed the big man.

'Where are we taking them to?' Enquired the big man. He was used to being in charge, but his fear of Si was palpable – Si could almost smell it.'

'Take A96 on way to Kintore,' he said, 'I tell you when to turn into freight park we use – you should find easy eh, you been policeman long time.'

Both men climbed up into the cab of the lorry. The engine gunned to a start, at low revs it vibrated fiercely. The driver carefully pulled away just as the first rays of sunlight pierced the horizon in the east, the fiery oranges and purple a promise of the day to come.

# Twenty

The Eurocopter 225 Super Puma is a long range helicopter its configuration provided space for 12 passengers together with an array of surveillance and forensic equipment. There was ample space for the forensic team together with Floyd and Becca who sat in the rear two seats offering them a degree of privacy. Floyd was amused at the deference all of the team seemed to show to Becca.

Becca showed Floyd how to operate the comms system so that they were able to have a secure conversation without being overheard by any of the team.

After the initial exhilaration of the huge machine being lifted skyward by the two Turbomeca Makila 2Ai Turboshaft engines powerfully thrusting against the constant force of gravity, Floyd settled into the flight. They rapidly gained altitude affording breathtaking views over the contrasting scenery below. As they flew south the Cairngorms could be seen rising to their right, hills capped with dense pine woodlands trailing towards the majestic peaks beyond, the snow line visible on the more distant Munros.

To their left the North Sea, peppered with supply vessels servicing the distant rigs and offshore installations. Picking up speed they began tracing the rugged coastline and Floyd recognised the dunes of St Cyrus beach as they trailed off to the town of Montrose and its huge tidal basin.

'That's the beach down there where the body was washed up last week.' Floyd reflected out loud. 'I remember seeing it on the news at the time.'

'Yeah – body's still in the morgue waiting for release. He doesn't know it but he has played a big part, at least I hope, in Athena cutting the head off of this particular gang.'

But there was something snagging in Floyd's mind, something that he heard from the news reel that wasn't quite right. Unable to put his finger on it he sat back in the seat allowing the intense drone of the engines to have their hypnotic effect lulling him into a state of semi consciousness.

The helicopter touched down briefly on the periphery of Leeds Bradford airport, outside an anonymous looking hanger. The team disembarked together with the flight crew while ground staff refuelled the aircraft.

In no time Floyd and Becca were airborne once more, but this time they were the only passengers in the helicopter together with a new flight crew. Now on a south west bearing they were cruising at 160 miles per hour at an altitude of 17,000 feet.


It was early evening when they started to descend. The metallic voice of the co pilot breaking the reverie that both Floyd and Becca had fallen into over the past hour. Still at some height the traffic moving in both directions along the M4 motorway assumed the appearance of small toys.

'We'll be there in a couple of minutes, the pilot's going to drop us off on the playing fields of the school. Kind of surreal really after all this time.' She smiled ironically at him, brushing his forearm – a small show of affection immediately putting Floyd at ease.

'Ok,' he started, 'it'll only take us a few minutes to get down to Cherry Orchard where Doris lives. They'll probably be out at the reunion but we can wait in the house for them. I know where Doris keeps a spare key. I'm willing to bet that even after fifteen years it's in the same little hidey hole.'

Landing the helicopter on the football pitch was a piece of cake. Conditions were perfect and the school grounds were flat as well as conveniently located on the top of a hill. Becca and Floyd removed and replaced their head phones. Lowering the side door they both emerged quickly from the belly of the huge rumbling beast crouching low and running away from the powerful downdraught caused by the rotors. Once they were at a safe distance Becca made a series of thumbs up gestures to the pilot, who in turn rapidly took the machine back up leaving them in silence once more. Floyd grabbed Becca's hand. 'Come with me.'

As they walked briskly out of the school grounds heading down towards Cherry Orchard, a vista of the town opened up. The view of the houses punctuated by trees and greenery led the eye towards the high street in the centre of the town. From where they were they could only make out the towers of the two churches and Town Hall either end of the High Street. In a moment of emotion, Floyd felt the pang of loss, a childhood past, a Father now gone – life was full of forks in the road where choices have to be made. He felt a prickling of tears welling up behind his eyes.

'Ok, Beccs, this is it,' he declared as they walked down the road and then standing moments later in front of number thirty seven.

Doris's home was a modest semi-detached house, similar to most of the others along the sweeping road. Unlike most however number thirty seven appeared to be stuck in the time when it was built, no rear extensions, no UPVC double glazing and in the tiny driveway leading up to the brightly painted single garage was a pristine green Morris Minor Traveller.

'I'll knock first just in case they're still in, don't want to shock them too much by just walking in.' Floyd, paced to the front door and after a moment's pause knocked on the door.'

Calling over to Becca he said, 'the spare's in the glove compartment in the Traveller, in the glasses case.'

'You're kidding right, she leaves a house key in an unlocked car?' In only moments Becca was rummaging through the brick-a-brac in the glove compartment, until she found the key. 'Smells really doggy in there.' She announced puffing her cheeks out.

'Always does, she only really ever uses the Traveller for taking her dog out on its walks, keeps all of his things in the back. Always the same dog, too, and then it was sometimes two of them at a time, but always the little Pug – loves them to pieces she does. She's had eight of them now; apparently that's why this one is called Henry.'

'Here,' she said passing him the key, completely uninterested in an old lady's love of her dog: Floyd however always had a soft spot for the daft old bat and her little grunting dogs – he smiled at the thought of her as he gently opened the door, peering into the gloomy hallway.

'Doris,' he called out in a sing song voice, 'Mum,' a little louder.

Becca hustled in behind him getting antsy wanting to do what needed to be done – a woman of action, thought Floyd.

'You take the downstairs, Floyd, I'll quickly scout around upstairs.'

As if walking on egg shells Floyd stepped through into the living room to the left of the hallway calling out to any inhabitants. The room was the same familiar place, perhaps a little more cluttered than before, if indeed that were possible. Not knowing where to start Floyd absent-mindedly lifted the little ceramic figure off of the mantel. It was of a little boy and girl leaning together and kissing – Amsterdam – 'see you've been off on your travels Doris.' He smirked.

To the rear of the living room a doorway led to the kitchen. Plastic tassels of varying colours hanging in the doorway obscuring the view beyond.

Pushing forward and through the tassels Floyd halted and stood transfixed. At that moment it seemed as if the earth stop spinning on its axis – time stood still.

He didn't hear Becca calling to him announcing that all was clear upstairs. And then suddenly she was there next to him holding the tassels back to one side, following his gaze.

The lifeless body on the kitchen floor – a vessel where life had lived until this day. Thick congealed blood almost black now had pooled all over the floor beneath the woman's left arm – a single shot to the heart. The second shot passing under her chin had removed much of the back of her head – brain tissue, bone fragments splattered over the base of the cupboard. The second shot appeared to come from the direction of the door after the first shot to the heart had taken her down.

Floyd found his voice after what seemed an age. 'It's Doris!'

Taking a step backwards he halted at the sound coming from the back door beyond the scullery. He contemplated stepping over the body, but the space was limited and it just didn't seem right. Instead pushing past Becca Floyd stumbled back through the living room like a drunk doing his best to stay upright. He burst out of the front door pausing to get his bearings then dashed around the side of the house along the path that was obscured by thick hedging.

'Floyd,' Becca called worried at his reaction, but desperate not to draw attention. About to follow him around the back she almost bumped head on into him as he returned. In his arms was Henry, the little dog's bulbous eyes fixing on her as his laboured breathing came in and out in grunts, his tongue curling up to meet his flat nose.

'Get in the car.' She instructed. Ushering him in before he had too much time to think.

'Wait,' he said, getting out again. Carrying Henry with him he opened the rear doors which opened out sideways. Henry was now struggling, anxious to get into his crate in the rear of the car. He was always happy to get in the car since there would normally be a walk in the woods and lots of treats at the other end of the journey.

Getting into the passenger's seat of the small car but without turning to look at Becca he said. 'Surely Yvette wouldn't do such a thing?'

Becca turned the ignition using the key that she had lifted from the kitchen. Reversing carefully out of the driveway she found first gear and gently pulled away.

They drove along the road in silence both of their minds racing.

'Do you still have the iPhone locator set up on your mobile Floyd? Why don't you see if you can find where she is.'

'Just pull over a moment.' He shook himself to clear his head, still talking as he punched instructions into his phone. 'Poor Doris, but what about Mum, she was here just a few hours ago, I spoke with her – I doubt she would go off somewhere on her own without Doris.'

'Yeah I was thinking along the same lines, but I guess if they wanted to harm your Mum then they would have done it by now. We've got to find them, any luck with that thing?'

'No, she must have set it to private, either that or her phone's off.' He tossed the phone into the glove compartment on top of Doris's old spectacle case. 'So what do we do now? He asked rubbing his temples with two fingers trying to relieve the tension headache that he could feel developing.

'Right, Ok well we do have one thing going for us and that's the element of surprise. For the time being I'm heading out of town, this car is far too recognisable, the killer must have walked right past it going into and out of Doris's house, so chances are if we get seen they'll put two and two together. I need you to navigate – what's the quickest way out of town to a quiet spot?'

The little Morris Traveller purred down the hill away from the school.

'Take a right at the junction, then go over the mini roundabout and straight on.' He guided her out of the town and after about five minutes they were on the Salisbury road surrounded by the trees of Savernake Forest.

'OK, see that small turning over there on the right,' he instructed. That heads down to Wootton Rivers.

She followed his instruction turning right. They then pulled into a lonely Forestry Commission picnic site immediately on their left. Becca reversed the car into the shadows but facing the entrance of the site. Anyone driving in would barely make out the car in the dwindling daylight let alone its occupants. She switched off the lights and killed the engine.

# Twenty one

Floyd stared vacantly out of the front windscreen of the Morris. The glass was steaming up from his and Becca's warm breath, the glass being cooled from the outside as the temperature dipped further. They had been there for the best part of forty five minutes by which time it had become almost pitch black outside. Only the occasional car passing by could be seen, probably heading into town thought Floyd, allowing himself to think of such normality.

Becca had been working the phone all the while seeking an update from the forensics team being especially interested in whether they had broken the encryption key on the chip. The one-sided dialogue suddenly registering through the fog of Floyd's mind.

'The chip is our best chance of locating all of their captives. I want a coordinated strike once we decrypt.' She listened intently to the other party of the call. 'I know using decryption is a process of brute force, so if you're telling me we don't have enough computing power to do the job get Ivan to hijack the CERN network. Call me when you get something.'

'OK big shot, so what do we do now?' He struggled to prevent the hostility he was feeling from escaping in his voice. 'Sorry,' he said. 'I know you have a responsibility to all of those people they've got locked up somewhere, and I don't want to sound cruel, but right now all I can think of is my mum.'

He pulled the latch on the door.

'Hang on a minute,' she barked into the phone and turning to Floyd 'where are you going?'

'Just taking Henry out poor little thing's just about crossing his legs back there. I could use the fresh air as well – clear my head.'

Putting Henry down onto the woodland floor the little dog trotted away but never letting Floyd too far out of his sight. Snuffling around at the base of a nearby tree he seemed to find an interesting scent and after a little more toing and froing relieved himself over a tuft of course grass.

'I'm sorry, little fella, it's been a terrible day for you. The least I can do is look after you – alright … would you like that?'


Becca was trying to wrap up her call when Floyd frantically pulled the door open holding an object out desperately trying to find the words. Henry, with his front two legs now on the ledge of the car and his hind legs on the ground was also staring up at Becca. Two sets of eyes imploring her for attention.

'Got to go.' She ended her call.

'What is it, guys?' She couldn't help a cheeky grin seeing the double act. 'Looks like you two boys have been bonding nicely.'

'J—Just got another email through! He exclaimed …'Same address as before. you know the watchingoutforyou@gmail.com address. It must be them.'

'What does it say?'

'Hang on, I haven't opened it yet, I er, sorry my hands are shaking like a leaf.'

Floyd sat down on the passenger seat passing the iPhone over to Becca. Henry bounded up onto Floyd's lap making himself at home. Becca reached for the ignition and started the engine then switched on the heater to try and warm them up a little..

'Close the door.' It's getting cold. She said, now opening the email to read.

'It says … *"You don't know me but I have been able to help your Mother out of a difficult situation. Don't worry she is safe. Can we talk urgently? Skype me on this address as soon as possible. We need to talk!"* … Well, if this is an email from Yvette, then who killed Doris? It doesn't make any sense – we know Yvette is up to her neck in the trafficking ring so she doesn't strike me as the good Samaritan type.

'Well let's Skype that address see who we are dealing with. Agreed?' Suggested Floyd.

'You're right we don't have anything else to go on at the moment … do it!'

He located the App on his phone. Opening it he typed in the address. Becca controlled her impatience at his slow finger movements. A pause followed by a musical series of tones as the messaging system connected, hailing their mystery person to pick up.

The screen flashed the image of the person initially dark as the lens adjusted to the inside light level. After a second or two the image became clear, albeit the movements were lagging.

The person looking at Floyd through the screen on his phone was completely unknown to him. He had half expected to recognise him, for the pieces to start falling into place.

Only the man's head and shoulders were visible. A middle aged man of Asian appearance, it was clear, nevertheless, that he was not a big man, not small, but lean and compact, very smartly presented in a formal navy blue jacket, a clean white collared shirt and tie. A man in whom precision was valued. As he spoke his words were clear and precise, too.

'Hello Mr Carter,' he started, 'I am so glad that you have contacted me. 'You must be wondering what sort of trouble your Mother has been getting into?'

Becca peered into the screen careful to remain out of view, a spark of recognition tugging in the back of her mind, unable however to grasp that particular thread.

'Where is she, what have you done with my mother?' Floyd hissed.

'She's fine. She's freshening up at the moment ...'

'I saw what you did to Doris, you monster ...' almost yelling now, 'If you harm one hair on her head, so help me God I'll kill you.'

'Whoa there Mr Carter, nobody is going to harm your Mother...ah, I see what is happening,' he declared seeming to work something out.

'Yes, I see, Mr Carter, so you have been to the house in Cherry Orchard, is that Doris's little dog I hear with you. Such a tragedy,' he paused, 'so, Mr Carter, are you still in Marlborough right now? I thought you were in Aberdeen?'

'Near enough, but look before we go any further I don't know you and I still want to see that Mum is safe and well.'

'Of course you do, Mr Carter, how rude of me, let me introduce myself. My name is Sim Li Wei, please call me Li Wei. I was your Father's personal assistant. Ah here she is.'

Floyd's mouth hung open watching his Mother appear through the door behind Li Wei – her face coming into focus as she approached the screen. She sat next to Li Wei looking into the camera and directly at Floyd.

'Oh, my Dear, you're safe, I've been so worried about you.' Her face was etched with worry lines deeply burdened by the events of the day and the realisation that her carefully constructed peaceful existence had been shattered – and worst of all the very real possibility of harm coming to her only son.

'Mr Carter,' Li Wei interjected, we are close by so I think perhaps it would be wise to meet up. I am sure that you would be pleased to see your mother, yes?'

Nothing made sense who was this man; his Dad was a fabricator and never mentioned anything about there being a secretary or personal assistant.

'Floyd, listen to me,' his mother cut in, 'it's ok, honest I'm safe now, thanks to Li Wei, he had nothing to do ...' she crumbled for a moment thinking of her old friend, she continued through her tears, 'he didn't harm Doris, if—if it weren't for him I would have been killed too for sure.'

'Mr Carter, please, you need to come here for there is much that you need to know.' Li Wei, gave Floyd an address and instructions on how to find them.

'OK I expect I can get there within the hour – no tricks.'

'Of course.'

Floyd turned to Becca. 'Right Becca, swap over I'm driving.'

Floyd got out of the car and put Henry back into his crate in the boot. He then returned getting into the driver's seat.

'Right, I know exactly where it is that he is taking us and if we get a move on we'll be there in less than an hour. At the moment I still don't trust him, so let's let him think that it's just me, and Henry of course. Give you chance to slip around the back.'

'You're starting to think like one of my guys now, Floyd, where are we going?' She allowed her gloved hand to rest for a moment on his left thigh as he revved the engine, lifted the clutch and pulled away.

# Twenty two

It was late by now and she had anticipated getting the job done earlier and then heading straight back up north. There were flights later in the evening that they could have taken from Heathrow. The Trustee had indulged her in allowing her to keep him alive since it was the only way to find Doreen. But this had taken too long and too much was at stake. And while the Trustee was willing to allow Yvette to eliminate Doreen, she was becoming a loose end herself now after all; it was Floyd who was the primary objective and she had lost sight of that.

'Ah, my dear little avenging angel,' Si lounged on the bed in a hotel room, methodically disassembling his pistol and lovingly cleaning each and every component in turn. 'Do not take it so hard, there will be another day. But you know we must get back and kill Carter – I have just had the SMS from the Trustee, he says we must get back and do it – no more delays. Besides we cannot leave the stock to perish no?'

As she paced the room her rage only intensified – she was a coiled snake about to strike at any moment.

'She was there, you fucking idiot,' she exploded, 'she was there and you just had to go and blow the old bitch away before we had her ... You know what, I have absolutely no intention of leaving here until I get what I came for so why don't you just piss off back up there and stiff him yourself if you're so keen on pleasing the Trustee?'

Si smiled, if he had to he would, but the Trustee was concerned about Yvette. "Another loose end." He had said to Si in that Texan drawl, a thread that was unravelling that needed to be tidied up. She had done her job well flushing out the heir to his co-Trustee, but she was questioning his authority now with these delays. It couldn't be tolerated.

'Get me a whisky.' She demanded.

Si placed the now reassembled gun on the bedside table, swinging around and stepping over to the mini bar under the desk. In silence he carefully prepared two tumblers of whisky. He reached out his hand passing the whisky to her and as she approached him to take the drink he could detect the darkness in her eyes. He had seen it before – the gaze of a predator, cold determination and a frisson of sexual electricity if he was not mistaken.

She drank the amber spirit in one throwing the glass against the wall in the far corner of the room shattering it into a million splinters. He could now see her breasts heaving, straining against the low slung neckline of her blouse, her heavy breathing betraying the instinct – rage, anger, hate never far from the lust that was now also rising to the surface.

As she grabbed the buckle of his belt she began greedily undoing his trousers threading the belt all the way out of his jeans. Desperate now, she fumbled with his buttons releasing him, his desire growing visibly. Fiercely she shoved him hard with both hands and he fell backwards onto the bed, his trousers now having found their way right down around his ankles. The sudden loss of balance surprising Si and catching him off guard. 'Easy, my angel ...'

'Shut the fuck up, you piece of shit, now you're gonna get what's coming to you.' A look of consternation broke out on Si's face at the aggression in her voice, but as she straddled him reaching down and pulling her panties to one side, he could only surrender to the promise of erotic pleasure.

Wasting no time she then impaled herself viscously onto the Slav's manhood wildly bucking backwards and forwards a balloon of need swelling in her belly – a sweet agony desperate for release.

It happened so quickly, that he had no chance whatsoever of seeing death being visited upon him, far less the chance to do anything about it. As her body convulsed through a shattering climax – in a single rapid movement unseen by Si as his eyes were rolling back into his head as he approached his own peak, she withdrew a long hairpin from the bundle of hair held in place on the top off her crown. Swooping the six inch spike in an over hand arc she brought the pin home to rest piercing Si's left eye, passing through the frontal cortex of his brain and ending its journey at the back of his cerebrum a centimetre from the rear of his skull. Death was instant as the passage of the weapon caused massive trauma to multiple critical centres necessary for brain function. Si's autonomic reflex response, however, continuing to function post mortem causing him seconds later to ejaculate deep inside Yvette – he twitched like a condemned man hanging from a noose. With a groan of intense pleasure she leaned forward and kissed the dead man deeply on the lips sliding her tongue into his mouth hungrily, her hips squirming on his body like a parasite draining its host of its last dregs of life force.


After a long, relaxing shower Yvette prepared for bed carefully applying her body lotion, a dab of expensive perfume and slipping into her purple silk nightwear. Sleep would be welcome; after all she needed to be even more determined to accomplish her goal with utmost haste before leaving to return north of the border. She returned to the bed and slid between the sheets noticing and enjoying the thrill of the cool cotton against her skin – the tingle of goose flesh.

As sleep crowded in she threaded her arms around Si's torso, still some residual heat, but cooling slowly. She snuggled up tenderly kissing his shoulder a purring sound barely audible in her contentment.

# Twenty three

The Morris Traveller maintained a steady speed west along the A4 having driven through the double width high street in Marlborough minutes before. The road was wide and punctuated with turns and peaks making for hard work as Floyd shifted up and down through the gears.

The clear full moon bathed the fields in an otherworldly dim light casting the silhouette of Silbury Hill against the sky. A spectacular construction built by Neolithic man resembling an inverted giant's bowl.

In the back Henry sat sentry peering over the edge of the rear windows unable to see anything other than his own reflection. The solitude suited all three of them equally well.

Breaking the silence Floyd said, 'OK we'll be there in a couple of minutes.' They took a sharp right off of the main road and another onto a small country lane. 'See that house there,' he pointed, 'on the far side of that large Sarsen Stone see the hedging, it's in there – should be easy enough for you to get through. I'll phone you and leave my phone switched on in my shirt pocket, that way you'll be able to hear what's going on.

'OK, sounds like a plan Floyd,' Becca yanked the door open, 'give me five minutes to get across the field and into position. Guess you'll have to make your way back around the main road. You still got the Sig?'

'Yeah, all set …' he said starting to doubt himself.

He manoeuvred the car in the field gateway turning round and heading away Becca found herself giving a little wave to the Pug gazing at her in the rear window mist blossoming on the glass with each breath.

Floyd swung the little car brutally around the roundabout along the road, tall hawthorn bushes flanking on either side. Suddenly the road opening out as it swung left into the village of Avebury nestled within the ring of ancient Neolithic stones and earthworks.

As he travelled along the road threading through the village he passed the Red Lion public house. Floyd recalled happier carefree times when, as teenagers, he and his mates would cycle over here in the long summer days after their A levels dreaming of their futures. Now in the small hours, the place appearing barren and completely deserted, those days seemed a lifetime ago. Instead driving through the night the monotone colour of the landscape a reminder of serious matters and serious people: Floyd didn't belong here he wanted to be that boy again where the days were a palate of brilliant colours – the future not yet written.

Heading through the gated entrance the car slowly crawled along the narrow gravel drive, its wheels crunching and announcing his arrival. Better give her a few more moments to get into a good position he thought, taking his time to get Henry out of the back. Sifting through the clutter in the boot Floyd looked around for a lead or something to improvise as one. Henry now stared up at him with longing – perhaps there was no need for the lead, he thought; Floyd now realising that the little dog was his shadow and wouldn't leave his side.

The eighteenth century rectory sat within a large garden fringed with tall beech wood hedging. It was a double fronted house with large sash windows its thick curtains were drawn keeping all of the light within. There were no external lights illuminated, but in the full moon Floyd's eyes adjusted with ease. He lifted the door knocker and knocked firmly.

'Oh Floyd,' the door flew open revealing his mother who threw herself at him embracing him in a bear hug. 'I'm so pleased that you are here and that you're alright,' her voice quivered, 'it's been terrible, just awful; poor Doris.'

Floyd placed his arm protectively around her shoulder and ushered her back into the hallway its warm light spilling out onto the front drive. Henry trotted happily behind in their wake. Li Wei stood at the end of the hallway keeping his distance while Floyd and his mother were reunited.

Li Wei made a small coughing noise at the other side of the hall to make his presence known while Henry stood protectively in front of Floyd and Doreen and barked three or four times to make a point, but lacking commitment.

Bowing slightly, Li Wei said 'Mr Carter I cannot tell you how honoured I am to have you here and so pleased that you are safe and well. These are troubling times are they not?'

Floyd is immediately thrown by Li Wei's formality, but dismisses it just as quickly as being his way. Now without a jacket it is clear that he is a small man in his slacks, white collared shirt and club tie.

'Please will you join me in the drawing room, Mr Carter, I know it is very late and you must need your sleep but Mrs Carter and I must speak with you before you retire.'

Remembering Becca he pulled his telephone out of his breast pocket and holds up his hand as he spoke into the phone.

'Becca, it's me all's well just come around the front.' He put his hand down, 'sorry, eh, thought it sensible to take precautions.

'Very wise, Mr Carter,' said Li Wei nodding with approval.

Floyd, stepped into the hall in order to let Becca in and then led her into the drawing room to join the rest of them.

'You remember Becca don't you, Mum?'

It took a moment but there was the spark of recognition lighting up his mother's face.

'Becca my dear, my goodness you have changed, b— but,' she struggled to make sense of it, 'how on earth did you get wrapped up in all of this?'

Becca hugged the old woman fondly before stepping back and lowering herself into the floral sofa next to the open fire that was crackling away. The others took her queue other than Li Wei who, the perfect host that he was, poured generous measures of brandy into glasses passing them first to the ladies and then for Floyd and one for himself.

'May I propose a quick toast,' said Li Wei. 'All will become clear shortly, but I'd like to drink to your Father Floyd, the Trustee whom I have had the honour to serve for over thirty years. Doreen, Floyd I toast your good health too, and lastly Rebecca Atworth, Commander in Chief of Unit 45, Athena – it is an honour, I salute you.' He lifted his crystal brandy glass and took a sip.

Becca stared at the man with incredulity.

# Twenty four

'Please, Ms Atworth, let me try to help make sense of the events that have been unfolding.' Turning to Mrs Carter, Floyd's mother, Li Wei continued in his apologetic tone, 'Doreen, I know that it might be painful but it is important that they understand what has transpired in the past; it is the key to understanding why all of this is happening now. At least some of it, much still remains unclear even to me.'

Li Wei leaned in towards the fire and picked up a poker from the companion set. As he prodded the embers in the grate the flames caught and licked higher illuminating that side of his face, while the other side remained cast in shadows.

Looking for the right place to begin he said, 'The Foundation started life in the late eighteenth century by the three founding families just as the industrial revolution literally exploded across the globe. The Founders were shrewd individuals who, seeing the way that the wind was blowing, collectively built interests in many new industries. The world was a very different place then under the reign of King George III. With the Boston Tea Party and troubles in the American colonies, revolutions in France many opportunities arose in both legitimate and illegitimate ways for an ambitious forward-looking organisation – which the Founders most certainly were. The Founders expanded their footprint across countries and continents following the growth of populations and fortunes building a large and expanding empire.

The organisation became known as The Foundation. Its interests being as diverse as you can imagine: Land, financial institutions, manufacturing....'

'Not to mention extortion, arms dealing, drugs and prostitution ...' cut in Becca, a red flush rising in her cheeks betraying her anger.'

Li Wei, gently held out his hands turning his palms upwards and with a slight nod of acknowledgement continued ... 'It is, as you say, Ms Atworth, not all the most pleasant of occupations and indeed as nations have fought nations, since the very earliest days of The Foundation, governments have turned to us for military support, strategic intervention even contract espionage. The British Government are a prime user of many of our services. And yes The Foundation has been involved with every vice of humanity catering to its needs. Many of our activities may appear unpalatable to many people, and yet we have not been wholly motivated by greed and power. The Founders and their successors have for over a hundred years fostered very close relations with the principal governments and societies of the elite. Humanity is a very complex system needing to be guided and engineered by benign leadership which, because of mankind's inherent dysfunctional character, must be undemocratic and most important – secret.' Seeing Becca's increasing exasperation Li Wei decide to change tack.

'I know that Athena do not see things this way, please I am but a mere servant of my Master. There will be plenty of time to debate the rights and wrongs.' Turning to Floyd, Li Wei stared intently as if willing him to understand. 'The Foundation has for many years been a huge empire, a prime figure in the unseen elite structures of first world development and social engineering. You will no doubt be familiar with the various conspiracy theories surrounding the Bilderburg Group, a group without formal membership with an annual meeting of the world's most influential thinkers and leaders?'

By now Floyd's mind was spinning, 'eh ... yes I think I've heard of that , what about it?' He looked Li Wei in the eyes trying to read not only what he was saying but what he was not saying. 'Go on ...'

'Well most people will tell you that is all there is to the Bilderburg Group after all, the agenda for the meetings together with the list of participants can be easily found each year on the internet. But that is only half the story.' Pausing Li Wei sank back into his wing-backed chair enjoying a long sip of brandy, now seeming to forget the company in the room. Seconds later he roused himself now turning his attention to Becca.

'It may surprise you Ms Atworth that the Bilderburg Group takes its name from the first meeting which happened in the Hotel Bilderburg in 1954 in The Netherlands. A coincidence that will perhaps not be lost on you?' He smiled as if consoling a child. 'You see, Ms Atworth, the need for social cohesion and controlling of the masses was recognised by both the Founders and governments. The Bilderburg Group simply being an outward expression of the collaboration of the elite in those changing times. Athena also came into being at that time based on the recommendations of the British intelligentsia seeing the need for an enforcer of last resort, above all politics and public scrutiny. You see it was the British Home Secretary at the time – Sir David Maxwell Fyfe, who created the charter for Athena. However since it was meant to be free from the medalling hands of politicians and deniability was desirable, an accord was struck with the Foundation to be the architects and financial springboard to the Unit. And so Unit 45, Athena, came into being.' He shrugged his shoulders, 'But of course that was then and this is now, once the Unit was up and running it took on a life of its own. At the time of the original charter the governments of the day agreed a certain latitude for the Foundation after all we were fellow elitists and really laws are only there for the masses to follow. A view which over subsequent years of liberal thought and the media taking a greater hold over the political debate it suits our governments to lean on their deniability. And since all of the key protagonists are long gone it is easier for people and politicians to paint the world into good guys and bad guys.'

Unable to contain herself any longer Becca exploded.

'What a crock of shit, I mean I've heard some things in my time. It's your organisation that pedals drugs, arms, prostitution and God knows what else and you're telling me that we're supposed to accept this?'

Li Wei stood up, surprisingly unshaken, moving towards the sofa he sat on the edge next to Doreen.

'No, I am not saying that, but life is complicated and my Master, Trustee Aldridge, is a good man. He has been seeking to influence the Foundation for betterment, from within. What I am saying is that after a full life of privilege and service to the Foundation Mr Paul Aldridge has been fighting his own long and difficult battle against Leukaemia. It is a battle that I am sorry to say will be lost very soon.'

As Li Wei looked at Doreen, he gently laid his hand on hers. She stared at him in disbelief. 'Paul … Paul Aldridge was one of these Trustees?' She gaped putting her hand over her mouth.'

'Yes he was, and I must tell Floyd the rest of the story with your permission Mrs Carter?' He asked in a low gentle tone.

'No, I'll tell them.' She said.

'I'm sorry, Floyd. It was all such a long time ago. We'd not long been married and times were tough trying to make ends meet, so to help make the bills I was doing some temping work through an agency, secretarial and administrative work wherever I was able to. It must have been in the autumn of 1985, when I got a placement as an administrator for Paul who was staying in a manor house outside Marlborough. I would cycle there every morning for the best part of a month. I spent a lot of time with Paul then, taking dictation, scheduling, filing … it was nice, he was nice, spoke to me like a human being even asked me what I thought about things. I had no idea what he did but I knew he was very important and that can make a young girl a bit giddy sometimes. It was a mistake I didn't plan it and neither did Paul. He was upset about something and I consoled him and ... well one thing led to another.'

Doreen looked at her hands which she was now wringing in her lap, embarrassed and ashamed.

'I'm sorry, Floyd, I was so ashamed at what I did, I left the agency immediately. I always meant to tell you, to some day let you know, but well I never knew how to ...' Her voice trailed away.

'Did Dad know? He asked mindful to not sound as if he was judging her.

'I never got around to telling him, which is why I never told you. But he's no fool, I think he knew, or at least suspected. I guess time just passed by and we left all that in the past, hoping that by not thinking about it then it wouldn't be real. What was real though, Floyd, was that we loved you very much, both of us.'

He felt he should get up and hug her, to tell her he forgave her. But he knew that was not her way.

'Thanks, Mum, that must have been hard to say. It's all OK.' He said.

'Let me explain why you needed to know this, Floyd.' Said Li Wei interjecting. 'The Foundation has a very strict constitution the third ownership of each Trustee can only be passed down the generation by bloodline from parent to their eldest child. If there are no children it reverts to the other two Trustees.' Everyone paid close attention.

'So, what happens if one of the remaining two Trustee dies without issue?' Asked Becca.

'In that case the whole dynasty is in the hands of the one, who will be the next Chairman. He or she must nominate two new Trustees to join them. For now, Floyd, what you need to appreciate are two very important facts. Firstly, when Master Aldridge dies, you will be his sole heir and as such will inherit all of his assets, titles and position as Trustee to the

133

Foundation.' The silence in the room was palpable just the crackle of the dimming fire in the grate could be heard.

'And what is the second fact?' Asked Doreen.

'Well the power and influence held by the Trustees is immense. Floyd, this is a time of great danger to you, it seems that one of your fellow Trustees desires that power for himself. If you were not in the picture to inherit the Trusteeship it would default to the other two. I believe the events we have seen recently are somehow tied in with at least one of the Trustees seeking to kill you for their own gain.

# Twenty five

By the time that the hotel's housekeeping had found the body Yvette was long gone having awoken in her room strangely refreshed and ready to renew her search. She had devoured a full English breakfast and downed two cups of strong coffee shortly after the restaurant had opened on the ground floor. Heading straight for the exit she waved demurely at the receptionist, who nodded politely in return.

'Thanks for the lovely stay; my partner will be checking us out when he gets up. It might be a while, he had more to drink last night than he's used to.' She shrugged, toying with the idea of making some witty remark about him having a splitting head. Amused by herself, she confidently swept her cashmere scarf over her shoulder heading out the door and to the car.

Time to take matters into her own hands she thought. She punched in a number on Si's mobile telephone that she had lifted from the jeans still wrapped around his ankles. She relaxed in the driver's seat of the car, the ringing tone now in her ear. She was in no hurry having left a "Do not disturb" sign on the bedroom door – it would be hours before Si's body was found.

'Si, it's Anderson here, everything alright?' She heard in the earpiece.

'Ah, Sergeant Anderson, unfortunately Si has had to leave on a rather long journey so you will have to deal directly with me from now on now.' She instructed.

He didn't need to ask who it was having met her on a number of occasions. Even though all of his dealings had been with Si, it was clear that Si was always led by her and so he needed to know what was good for him, too.

'Yes, Miss Semple, I see, so what is it you need, things are getting a bit hot at the moment with the John Doe case an' all so I do need to keep a bit of a low profile – is it the recent load,' he enquired, 'do you need me to check in on them and top them up, is that it?'

'Actually no, Sergeant. And you know, I don't remember you keeping a low profile when our mutual benefactor agreed to pay you a retainer for your services. As it happens it quite suits my needs to withhold provisions at the moment, never know when you might need some extra leverage. No, what I want from you is to locate the position of a mobile telephone. I'll text you the number – alright, and I want an address and postcode in under five minutes.' She barked her orders.

'Miss Semple, hang on a minute, while we don't need a warrant I will still need a senior officer's approval and I really ...'

She cut in hissing into the phone. 'Sergeant Anderson you're in this up to you fucking neck, and I'm sure you wouldn't want your precious daughter Lucy seeing you being carted off to Craiginches now would you? So I suggest you think of a suitable pretext and get me what I need – no excuses. Have I made myself clear?' She hung up not waiting for a response.

A second or two passed, Yvette recomposed herself flipping down the sun visor in the car. Surveying her face she clipped open her handbag retrieved a tube of bright red lipstick and carefully reapplied her colouring.

Satisfied with the touch up, she then smiled at herself in the mirror and placed the handbag into the passenger well of the car.

She eventually started the motor and pulled out onto the High street turning left into the one way system. Her spirits were high as she edged along the picturesque town centre another bright day it seemed as if the gods were smiling on her sending her their approval. She switched on the radio punching the scan button a few times until she found a channel with upbeat music to match her mood.

Aware of the time and knowing that she would have a few minutes to kill, as well as not wanting to drive too far unnecessarily, she flipped her indicator right and pulled into a parking slot in the centre on the High street. Normally drivers would have to trail for ages to find a spot, but a Sunday morning saw no such problems. Spotting the newsagents opposite Yvette cantered across the road and gently pushed the door open accompanied by a bell ringing on a spring above the door. It took a moment for her eyes to adjust to the gloomy interior. Immediately to her right were ceiling to floor shelves stacked with an assortment of newspapers, magazines and all manner of reading material. The two piles of Sunday papers were still on the floor, one was still bound with string unopened. She walked in letting her eyes rest momentarily on the confectionery then turning to the young man who was sitting behind the counter at the far end of the shop. He couldn't have been much more than sixteen years old an adolescent uncomfortable within his own form, and with the possibility of encountering this beautiful and strong woman his appearance seemed to diminish even further. Yvette walked towards him so he stood up off of the stool smoothing his right hand along his greasy hair and pushing it to one side in a vain attempt to conceal a cluster of acne on his left cheek.

'Can I help you, madam?' He mumbled.

'Umm, well you might, I'm looking for some OS maps do you have any?' She asked.

"Oh yeah, they're just around the corner, at least all you could need for this neck of the woods.' He grinned a self-conscious smile, which faded as she turned her attention immediately away from him.

As another customer entered the shop she edged past him an old man, while making her way to the bookshelf. 'Come on, Anderson!' Her phone buzzed in her pocket which she retrieved – great an address and postcode. Scanning through the library of OS maps she was able to quickly locate the relevant one.

Approaching the youth who was just handing change over and a packet of rolling tobacco to the elderly customer Yvette asked, 'I wonder if you can do me a favour. You see I'm going sightseeing in Avebury today, could you point me in the right direction from here?'

A twenty minute drive west of Marlborough along the A4 saw Yvette pull into a small car park at the foot of Silbury Hill. Stepping out of the car she spread the OS map onto the bonnet holding it at either side with her gloved hands. There was very little wind.

The address that Anderson had texted appeared to be on the north side of the village of Avebury with a small copse behind the property. The copse itself was also adjacent to the Great Barn, a National Trust exhibit. Deciding on her approach she folded the map and walked around to the boot of the car which she opened with the key fob. She unlatched the suitcase which had been left at the hotel for her. She then looked carefully all around her before lifting the lid. There was only one other car in the park, a solitary rusty Fiesta, probably belonging to the two early morning ramblers that she could see scaling the sides of the ancient hill.

Happy that she was alone she opened the case and selected a Beretta together with two spare clips of ammo, which she slipped into her coat pocket. Also searching through its contents she withdrew a K bar combat knife in a leather sheath. She examined the razor sharp edge and her reflection on the blade her predatory instinct flooding her bloodstream with a rush of endorphins. An overwhelming sense of euphoria – Today's the day.

# Twenty six

'Mum, I'm finding this all a little too much to take in. Is it true?' Floyd stood in the kitchen at one end of the table hands planted firmly on the edge as if he was in danger of collapsing. Opposite him his mother sat nursing the remains of a cup of tea which had long been cold. 'I don't know how much of what Li Wei said was true but, I can tell you that what I told you was true – I'm so sorry, Floyd, I never meant you to find out like this.'

It was unlike his mother to look so crestfallen; always the strong one in the household it disturbed Floyd to see her this way.

'Mum,' he started getting her attention. 'It's OK I'm not judging you I know you have always done what you thought was right.'

'Thank you, Floyd, but, oh I don't know I guess I'd put it all away into a corner for such a long time you know, convinced myself that things were different.'

'This doesn't change anything, Mum, you have to believe that you're the same person and Dad was still my Dad.' He crossed the room to embrace his mother, 'it's going to be alright.'

Sitting next to her he became more stoical and business-like. 'Now,' he said, 'but that doesn't deal with our immediate problem namely that whoever it was who did that to Doris must have been somehow tied in with what Li Wei said about the Trustee's legacy.'

Henry skipped into the kitchen looking for his own breakfast and started fussing around Doreen's feet. She reached down towards him and gave him a little ruffle on his head.

'I'll see what I can find for the little mite.' She said pleased to busy herself. As Floyd searched the cupboards for coffee the two slipped into a companionable silence for a few minutes.

'You know it seems bizarre that anyone would come after you Mum just to get to me, do you think that Li Wei might have it wrong,' he pondered, 'could it be that you inherit the legacy? – Maybe Paul wanted to make amends or something after all these years?'

'I can't see it, Floyd, I didn't want to have anything to do with Paul ... and after all this time.' She toyed with the gold wedding ring on her ring finger as they were speaking.

'So what about you, Mum, is there any reason why somebody would want you to come to harm? Do you have any enemies?'

'No I don't,' her voice raising in pitch in her alarm, 'I always thought I was an open book, the only secret I've ever had you now know. All I've ever done in my life is to try to be a good wife and mother working part time, when I could, I was just an administrator and most of the time that was at your old school, you know all of this, Floyd.'

'There's nobody —' Doreen started. But before she could continue, Becca hurried into the room interrupting her. 'Listen, Floyd, Doreen, I've just been onto the Home Office. I've been trying to get a lead on the human trafficking gang that we've tied Yvette to. The bald guy that we saw up at the farm buildings Floyd, well we've been able to ID him. He's one Silvije Petrovic, an ex-Croatian hit man; he learned his grisly trade in the Balkans conflict. I've instructed an update of all of his biometrics across UK law enforcement agencies –

as soon as we get a hit on his whereabouts I'll issue the kill order.'

Doreen's hand went to her mouth unable to comprehend – her world was a gentle place. Li Wei walked into the room having heard the conversation and without words stood next to Doreen in solidarity placing his arm around her.

'What about Yvette? Asked Floyd pouring himself another coffee from the cafetiere.

'Well that's where we hit a bit of a wall, seems that our Miss Yvette Semple doesn't exist, we did a thorough cross-check against all agency databases and social networks – Nada, she doesn't exist.'

Floyd slumped into the spare kitchen chair trying to process what he could. 'But ...' He started.

'Easy, tiger,' Becca announced, pleased with herself as she continued to click away furiously on her Blackberry. 'I've just been knocking a few heads together at the Home Office and it seems that Yvette Semple was the new identity given to a psychiatric inmate released on lifelong license in 2008.' Turning to look at Doreen she continued, 'She was sentenced eighteen years earlier for the murder of an eight year old boy. But at that time she was known as Tanya Gleeson. I understand you were a witness at the trial Doreen!'

Doreen had told Floyd the story about Tanya Gleeson before. In the Carters' home it was infrequently spoken about being such an unpleasant episode, but at the same time since it was a couple of steps removed from the happy family it never really disturbed the peaceful rhythm in the household.

Both Floyd's and Doreen's faces froze as the seemingly irrelevant chapter from deep in their past was thrust centre stage alongside the current events.

'Thought that would get your attention.'

Other than the sound of the crows squawking in the treetops in the copse behind the garden there was complete silence in the room as they digested the bombshell that Becca had just dropped. Suddenly and without warning Henry's ears pricked up and with the ferocity of a much larger dog he bounded to the back door growling and scraping at it alarmingly.

# Twenty seven

Leaving the city behind him Lachlan Anderson navigated his way along the A96 passing the roundabout beyond Blackburn at speed. He had only picked up the brand new Range Rover Evoque a few weeks ago and fortunately he hadn't re-registered it yet with his personal number plate, so he hoped it wouldn't be as easily noticed.

Cresting over the top of the long incline the vista opened up before him, a vast open and green landscape punctuated by hedgerows and ploughed fields. Wind turbines littered on the horizon were all turning clockwise in unison, mildly hypnotic as he stared at them, tempting him to steer into the oncoming traffic.

As he pulled into the gravel covered storage area he had to switch on his wipers as the rain started to fall obscuring his vision. It was a very lonely spot but nevertheless he was still careful to reverse his car completely out of sight behind the Lylandeii and heaps of discarded rubble.

Lachlan never considered himself to be a bad person, after all when he joined the force he was proud to be on the side of the good guys. But life tends to get complicated over time and with experience comes insight and he saw that this world wasn't black and white, just an endless spectrum of grey. What he wanted most of all was to be respected and it's hard to be respected in this town, or at least in Lachlan's mind, unless you looked successful, the big man. By making the choices that he did it was too easy to make that first one little compromise, but then that one compromise led him easily to the next and the next and so on until they had taken him to a place where he couldn't back out. If you try dealing with the Devil, then this is where it gets you he thought.

He pulled the collar up around the neck of his workman's black jacket as the rain beat down harder on him. Fishing the key out of his pocket he slid it into the padlock on the metal freight container which unlocked easily with a clunk.

Pulling the release lever Lachlan heaved on the right side door opening it just wide enough to slip in. The smell inside hit him in the face its acidic tang clawing at the back of his throat making him retch and back up quickly out of the door. He gasped urgently to fill his lungs with clean air and took a moment to steady himself.

Sergeant Anderson furtively scanned the area and once he was certain that he wasn't going to lose the contents of his stomach and double sure the coast was clear he pulled and released both doors of the container throwing them wide open allowing the grey day's illumination to pour into the darkness.

The stench of human waste and vomit sought to force him to step back while the terrified inhabitants also shrunk back in their cages unable to see him as the light of day blinded them temporarily.

Lachlan started busying himself with the tasks in hand, attaching the hosepipe to the standby pipe behind the container. Back inside the container he hosed down the sides and underneath the crates doing his best to remove the vile seeping mess. Why have they left these poor creatures like this for so long – he fought the urge to pity them, all the while never making eye contact.

Eventually he brushed out the waste over the edge and then carefully shovelled it all up into a wheelbarrow to remove into the woods out back. Returning to the front he brought the hose pipe in again to top up their water containers.

'Only half fill them.' Miss Semple had said and as he looked up into the far corner of the container the red flashing

LED, an unblinking eye, sent a jolt of anger and fear passing through him knowing that with each step down this road these devils pull him deeper into the pit.

He'd done what he came here for; it was now time to leave. He was pulling on the door when a voice penetrated the fog of his despair. 'Please, sir, please we'll die in here, please take pity.'

Don't look he told himself, but as he brought the door around his eyes locked onto her face. He tore them away immediately. Anguish was searing through her trembling body. 'My name is Oksana please help me I know you are a good man that is why you do not look into our eyes – not like him.' Lachlan stopped, frozen, unable to turn his head still hoping to avoid looking at her again. He stared into infinity across the fields and through the veil of rain which was now falling freely down his fringe and into his eyes. He made no attempt to clear his face ashamed at his tears, ashamed at what he had become.

'I am sixteen years old and I live in Kiev, I want to go to University to read ...'

The pain of guilt speared him, but he knew that to do something, to deny that unblinking eye would take courage. He also knew that he was not a strong man. He closed the door on Oksana's pleading voice, pulling the levers to seal the container closed and padlocked the door.

Silence once more.

Sergeant Anderson sat back in his new Range Rover being careful to replace the covers on the driver's seat to prevent them from getting wet. Pulling out of the narrow lane and then turning back onto the dual carriageway he drove at speed along the A96 but instead of heading back into Aberdeen he simply wanted to put distance between him and the past. On impulse he headed in the opposite direction moving beyond Kintore as the dual carriageway reverted to a normal two way trunk road the Evoque threaded around the bends. Anderson reached out and smoothed the leather passenger seat with his left hand appreciating the craftsmanship for a moment. Then, as he allowed his eyes to settle on the rotating blades of the wind turbines high upon the hill like synchronised swimmers – his right foot squeezed down to the floor causing him to surge back in his seat. Lost in the swirling blades Anderson heaved the wheel fiercely to the right colliding the Evoque into the oncoming logging lorry with devastating force.

# Twenty eight

Yvette used her time wisely having parked a couple of hundred yards away at the National Trust exhibition. She was unconcerned about the possible aftermath and police investigation – incarceration was a price worth paying if it came to it.

From her vantage point she only needed to spend a few minutes in order to see that there were four people in the house that she had under surveillance.

She should have been pleased that both of her targets were together in the same place, at the same time. But her irritation surfaced as she watched, hidden in the copse, observing that all four of their party were now together in the kitchen which was located at the back of the house. That would make things more complicated. Willing the other two away from Doreen and Floyd, Yvette bit hard on her gloved hand unable to control the seeping red mist.

As a small scream of frustration escaped her, half a dozen black crows scattered from the thinning canopy above her in a melee of squawking which shocked her back into reality. Yvette dropped down onto her haunches – watching.

She didn't have to wait long when the back door to the left of the kitchen window clunked. It was an old wooden door with peeling green paint and much in need of some oil on its hinges. Somebody was pushing it open the hinges protesting with a long dry grinding. It was impossible to make out who had opened the door which was shrouded under a shadow from the rear porch and adjacent wood store. Squinting from the bright sun light Yvette caught a sudden movement in her peripheral vision followed by the high pitched yapping of the small pug-faced dog which bounded through the hedging and in her direction.

She pulled the K bar knife out of its protective sheath and almost laughed out loud as she lunged out and swiped the deadly blade at the small animal. The dog beat a fast retreat into nearby brambles and dense undergrowth whimpering and leaving a trail of blood behind him.

Yvette refocused. She had prepared well for this day pulling out a remote device from her pocket, momentarily toying with the switch. Hidden under the rear wheel arch of the black BMW, belonging to Li Wei, was the receiver attached to three blasting caps inserted into four pounds of C4 plastic explosive. Yvette had planted the diversion earlier in the morning choosing this car over the Morris as it sat adjacent to the lawn and so could be approached undetected without having to cross the noisy gravel drive.

The explosion was deafening creating a wall of noise shattering the silence of the Sunday morning as the BMW erupted into flames, black smoke blossoming up and out in all directions. The percussion of the blast ripped the car open like a tin can scattering car parts in all directions at high velocity and causing significant damage to the front of the house, the window of the study shattered and walls studded with shrapnel damage.


Becca, Floyd, his mother and Li Wei all found themselves cast on the floor in the kitchen not so much through the force of the blast, which was contained at the front of the property, but through the instinctive responses of Becca and Li Wei. Momentarily deafened Floyd was unable to comprehend the words Becca and Li Wei were mouthing at him and Doreen. Unable as he was to think on the spot he simply crawled his way over to his mother on the floor and sat there with her, both of them shocked into silence as Becca and Li Wei leapt into action checking out the blast and its immediate locus around the front of the house and driveway with their weapons drawn.

'Oh isn't that so sweet,' came a familiar voice from the kitchen doorway which was still open to the rear garden having been left open for Henry. 'You know, hon, I did say it was about time you introduced me to your mother,' she mocked, looming over the two of them, her face an expression of mock chastisement between lovers.

Try as he might Floyd was unable to gain any traction on the tiled kitchen floor as he tried to stand up; instead he pushed backwards, huddling in the corner alongside Doreen who was by now struggling to catch her breath.

Floyd drew in a sharp breath when he spotted the pistol in Yvette's right hand – a silencer attached to its end. Raising her hand she pointed the weapon straight at him.

'Back to back on the floor, do it now, don't think or you're dead.' She commanded.

'OK, OK.' Floyd managed to respond almost in resignation desperately trying to think of what he should do next.

Yvette violently lashed out with the butt of the pistol, first hitting Floyd on the head then rapidly bringing it down on Doreen, missing her head but instead crunching it viciously against her left cheek bone under her eye. Both were in a dazed state as Yvette expertly bound their hands together with plastic cable ties in a matter of seconds as they slumped back to back. Next she produced a length of grey duct tape from a roll, tearing it free with her teeth, winding and sticking it harshly around their necks holding them tightly together, making them gasp for breath. Two final strips of tape were used to seal their mouths.

As full consciousness struggled to return to Floyd he became increasingly aware of Yvette who was prowling around the two of them, but he was unable to lift up his head to see her face. His head was now bleeding freely from the crushing blow she had administered, sending waves of pain and nausea racking through his body. Despite drifting in and out of the present Floyd could feel the warmth of his mother's back pressed against his own; an echo of comfort from her warmth and proximity. It took Floyd a few moments to realise that Doreen was shuddering, fear gripping her, causing her to whimper uncontrollably.

'It's all clear,' Floyd could hear Li Wei's voice, 'but we've been compromised and need to get you out of here.'

Pushing the door open to the kitchen Li Wei immediately registered the scene before him, Floyd and Doreen trussed back to back and gagged, bathed in blood, with Doreen almost convulsing through shock in her distress. Unfortunately he was unable to move in time to do anything about what he saw and the three shots that spat out of Yvette's silenced Beretta, two hitting him in the chest a third tearing away the side of his neck severing his carotid artery – he was dead before he hit the floor.

Floyd could feel he was losing the battle against his own terror, tears mixing with his blood he twisted feverishly against his bindings, but they were completely unforgiving biting deep into his wrists. Still unable to see Yvette he sensed rather than knew she was crouching in front of Doreen, and through his wild struggling he could only hear fragments of words as the blood pounded in his ears.

Doreen stared into the eyes of the predator. The little girl who had many years before killed for the first time, stared back into her own eyes. She was going to die here today and she knew it.

'I'm going to kill him, too.' Yvette whispered, now so close she almost hissed into Doreen's ear. 'Look into my eyes Doreen.' Now almost in a gentle tone, 'easy now, calm down, that's better, ssshh.'

Doreen averted her eyes staring down into her lap. The sight she saw poured absolute fear into her soul, as Yvette was straddling the old lady she no longer held the pistol, which now lay on the floor at her side. Instead she held in her hands the vicious K bar knife, its tip pointing at Doreen's abdomen ahead of its savage serrated edge.

Still leaning over and whispering, Yvette's eyes held Doreen's. 'You deserve to die Doreen, you deserve to die for what you did to me and as you die I'm going to be right here looking into your eyes and you'll look into mine.'

Yvette started to apply pressure on the knife it's razor like edge piercing the fabric and skin with ease. The penetration held no pain for her to begin with, but very soon searing agony and panic racked through Doreen's body; she shuddered knowing this was it, unable to scream, to call for help, her alarm was trapped – no way out.

She could have simply thrust the blade in to kill her prey, but like certain other predators, Yvette savoured the culling as she pushed the blade deeper into the old woman's core, centimetre by centimetre all the while holding the handle of the blade tight to her own most intimate of places.

'I can see the light dimming in your eyes Doreen, you are mine now – I'll be the last thing that you ever see.' And then like a lover unable to stop at the point of climax she thrust the blade hard and deep again and again. The pool of blood covered the entire lower half of her own body and as she brought her hand up to brush a loose hair out of her face, leaving a trail of blood on her forehead, a single shot was fired from in the living room. The bullet found its mark in a fraction of a second, hitting Yvette in the back of her skull. Its hollow-point tip fragmented on impact, tearing apart her brain stem. Death was instant.

# Twenty nine

As consciousness slowly returned to Floyd he struggled to take in his surroundings. It was clearly a hospital of some description. He could see that he was attached to a monitor, a chart was hanging on the end of his bed and a drip, attached to a tube, was feeding a cocktail of nutrients and sedatives into his bloodstream, cloaking him in a fuzzy, artificial sense of well-being.

A hospital it was, but not of the NHS variety. As more information slowly filtered through he recognised a large plasma screen television hanging on the wall opposite and two easy armchairs made of leather on chrome legs. Very chic, very expensive. There were no windows to look out of but the air drifting over the skin of his face was cool, piped in through air conditioning ducts overhead and hidden by a false ceiling.

If he thought hard enough he knew he would be able to recall the events that took place in Avebury. The images that popped uninvited into his mind from time to time were horrific and so he made the effort not to recall, to surrender to the gentle hand of whatever drug was flowing in his system once again giving in to sleep.

The next time he woke up it was different, the room was the same as before but shrouded in darkness, only a dim, single light source from somewhere behind his bed cast shadows around the room. He was cold from the air conditioning now and as he ran his hands up over the top of his covers he tugged up at his bed sheets revealing only a typical thin green hospital gown.

As his eyes refocused across the room expecting to see two empty chairs he was taken by surprise to realise that in the chair on the right, immediately next to the door, was the outline of a person leaning back resting their head on the wall apparently sleeping.

'Who's that?' He croaked, realising just how dry his throat was. Searching around his bed he located the controls. He pressed the up tilt button, the bed immediately obeyed his command with a gentle buzz. Once upright, he poured a couple of inches of water in the tumbler on the bedside table and drank it all down greedily.

'Hello. Who is that?'

'Er ... Oh Floyd. How are you?' The voice enquired with genuine concern: It wasn't a voice that he recognised.

Rising from his seat he paced across the room passing from the shadows and into the light. The figure crossing the room was of a small rounded older gentleman, his small dark eyes were deep and penetrating but at the same time gentle and earnest. His hair was almost entirely white, receding on his head it was elegantly trimmed and combed back. A neatly trimmed goatee beard hiding, but only just, a sizeable double chin together with a flamboyant dicky bow and tweed three piece suit rounded him off.

'I do hope I didn't wake you, dear boy, he said resting a pudgy hand on Floyd's arm. I wanted to be here as soon as the doctors started to reduce the sedative. I'm afraid I just sat down for a moment and was out like a light.'

'Who are you?' Floyd asked, now gathering his wits about him. He was becoming more alert by the minute and so it was only to be expected that he would become more anxious, but the man in front of him appeared both genuine and kind. Floyd relaxed a little.

'Of course, of course you must have so many questions and I will do my very best to answer them in due course. But for now, what you need to know is that you are in a medical facility held by Trustee Aldridge's branch of the Foundation. I'm Thomas, I am ... I mean I was Li Wei's under-secretary,' he paused for a moment looking at the floor taking a moment, 'such a waste, dreadful, just dreadful and I am so sorry about your Mother Floyd; I had the pleasure of meeting her once many years ago you know – lovely lady.' He muttered under his breath.

After his moment of reflection he rallied. 'I'm sorry Floyd but there are matters that we will need to discuss concerning the future of the Foundation. But before that there are a couple of visitors I think you might like to see.' He turned on his heels about to head for the door.

'Wait, please Thomas ... how long have I been here. For that matter, where, is here?' Floyd asked.

'All in good time, young man.' And with that Thomas pushed the door open beckoning to the unseen visitors.

Floyd was delighted to see Becca. Henry, always two steps ahead of her, leapt up onto the bedside chair and then up onto the bed and then immediately up onto Floyd's lap. He was sore from the experience of the day before and his heart felt so heavy for his mother, but seeing Henry's enthusiasm he couldn't help but smile a little.

After the hugging, Becca made small talk for a moment or two; then, satisfied that Thomas was gone, she backed up.

'Floyd, I can't tell you how happy I am that you are still alive – I really thought she'd done you in. What can I say, if only I'd returned a couple of seconds sooner I—'

'Beccs, it's OK, it wasn't your fault,' he interrupted, 'if it was anybody's fault it was mine. It was me who left the back door open. You know what, though, Beccs, at some point what happened to Mum is going to hit me like a train, but right now

I'm just gonna let this baby,' he pointed at the IV drip, 'keep me sane and try not to think about it for a while.'

'Suits me.' She said.

Taking a step towards the bed she perched herself on the side.

'Listen Floyd I have to get back to Aberdeen, we were able to access Yvette's phone and found a live web feed of the inside of the lock up with their victims. Looks like there are five of them and, well I guess you don't need the details but we have to figure out where they are otherwise there are going to be more bodies in the morgue ... sorry.'

'How are you going to find them?'

'Well the bad news is that we've not been able to decrypt their devices yet, but we got a break and have been able to track some of her recent calls which should get us close by.'

'Go get 'em, tiger.' He grinned a cheeky smile. 'You know, though, I can't help but think from what Li Wei told us that there are parts of the Foundation that would want to work with your organisation, to clear the rot out so to speak ... you were pretty hostile to him back there you know.'

Floyd cast his mind back to a time when he and Becca could really talk with each other, often about nothing whatsoever and other times about the heavy stuff, putting the world to rights they said. 'Don't you see Becca we can make a difference here, do some good in the world.' He willed her with his eyes, but something had changed. As Becca withdrew her hand from his arm he could sense the static forming in the air around them. A shadow formed across her features as she turned away from him preferring to stand at the end of the bed, out of reach, both feet firmly planted on the ground, while at the same time still a surly teenager with heavy make-up, tattoos, and body piercings.

'What do you mean do some good, that's exactly what I've been doing at Athena,' she grabbed the end of the bed leaning forward.

'Listen, Floyd, I hope you're not getting your head turned with all of this talk of legacies. Need I remind you that despite all of Li Wei's flowery words the Foundation is all about power and corruption, for goodness sake, you've seen firsthand its tolerance of modern day slavery in its ranks.'

'But isn't that the point?' he responded, 'you know also that more can be done from inside than as an outsider.'

'It's not the bloody EU you know, and besides I can't believe you're talking like this.'

'Come on, Beccs …' He started, but unable to finish as she cut across him, her voice betraying her increasing anger.

'Oh come on yourself, Floyd, don't play the frigging idiot, it's only natural, I mean you're looking at this as a chance to reinvent yourself, to get away from your dreary day job dealing with memos, tax returns and the underachieving corporate sociopaths bent on intimidation; I mean I get it. But this is not the answer, do something else anything. Because trust me, this is a one way street, the Foundation is no friend of yours … and it's no friend of Athena's.'

'Oh c'mon, Beccs, I think you're making too much of this.'

'No it's pretty straight forward,' now stepping towards the door she turned, 'look I've got to go, so you need to think about this long and hard, Floyd Carter, Athena are going to be all over the Foundation so you need to choose sides it's all or nothing.' She pushed the door open so ferociously that it crashed hard against the wall outside.

'Come on then, Henry, time to go!' She called from somewhere along the corridor.

The little dog turned to face the direction of her voice, but remained still on the bed not making a move.

'Suit yourself,' she said and with that she strode meaningfully away and out of Floyd's life once again.

# Thirty

The first thing that Floyd saw when he awoke some hours later was the nurse, a burly woman in a prim, white, starched uniform and cap as she wheeled in a trolley containing a covered plate and a jug of fruit juice together with a glass. The sedative must still be doing its job, he thought, – going out like a light like that.

He smiled at the nurse as she fussed over his bed helping him into a position where he would be able to eat comfortably.

'Thanks, nurse,' he said as she removed the covers from the food revealing a delicious pasta dish, the aroma reaching up to him causing his mouth to water. It only then struck Floyd just how hungry he was.

'You're welcome, Mr Carter, but I don't think it's a very good idea to keep your dog in here,' she admonished him, nodding towards Henry who had settled into one of the leather chairs, himself only just rousing from slumber.

'Oh I don't think that will be too much of a problem sister,' boomed Thomas's voice as he strolled through the doorway, 'and how is the patient this fine morning?' He asked.

'All the better for this.' Floyd spoke with his mouth full of pasta, gesturing at the bowl with his fork.

'In fact, I was thinking you might like to take Henry out for a little stroll this morning if you're feeling up to it?' Suggested Thomas walking towards the bedside his thumbs parked in the small pockets of his waistcoat. 'Besides, I'd like to introduce you to someone.'

The clouds raced across the sky, high and white, not threatening to rain. The wind danced around the open terrace picking up fallen brown leaves pushing them playfully in its eddies. The bright sunshine hung low in the autumnal sky occasionally dimming with the passing clouds only to be revealed again after a few seconds returning with the warmth carried on its rays.

Floyd and Thomas ambled through the French windows of the main house. The private convalescence home where he had been recovering over the past days was a combination of the contemporary medical wing, which had been sympathetically designed to complement the grandeur of the main building, itself a Jacobean hall built of red clay bricks and mullion stone windows. It was a patchwork of oranges, reds and brown, littering the skyline with chimneys, towers and parapets in an eclectic collection of parts working together and then sweeping down to the side of the terrace where the low slung buildings were clearly used as bedrooms for other residents, colourful curtains adorning the windows.

'This is a lovely place.' Floyd ventured to Thomas as they meandered companionably down the stone steps and onto the pathway that bisected the lawn.

'But whereabouts are we?'

'Just outside Chobham, in Surrey. It's just one of the many such facilities that the Foundation provides for the deserving and needy. As well as providing convalescence facilities it's also a hospice for the terminally ill.'

'And am I a prisoner here?'

Thomas stopped and turned to Floyd his eyes alive with humour. He chuckled.

'Oh my dear boy, neither you nor I or anybody else here for that matter are prisoners. Honestly, you are free to come and go as you please. I'm sorry that I am laughing, I guess I should have expected that – with Ms Atworth having spent some considerable time with you I am sure you have a very jaded view of the Foundation.'

'Becca and I go back a long way, I trust her she was always there for me when we were younger.'

Thomas shrugged. 'Listen, Mr Carter, I'm sure a lot of what Ms Atworth says is right and that's exactly why the Foundation needs to be transformed. But we are all no longer children and if you'll forgive me from quoting from the Bible, … we no longer think like children and must put our childish ways behind us … it's a very complicated world out there …' he flapped his hand as if dismissing his own words.

'But listen to me, you'll make up your own mind but I must warn you the time will come very soon when that decision has to be made one way or the other. Once any of the Trustees die, there is an administrative period during which time the personal assistant to the deceased Trustee will be their proxy, and in this case it will be the under-secretary … that'll be me. Proxy will extend for a period of one month. If the heir to the Trustee is not competent at that time then everything passes absolutely and irrevocably to the remaining Trustees.'

The two men having followed the path beyond the lawn then passed through a small walled garden containing borders of shrubs and flowers still displaying vivid colours despite the time of year. Emerging from the garden a still lake opened up in front of them flanked on all sides by deciduous woodlands. On a flat expanse a few yards from the edge of the lake was an odd assortment of people surrounding a medical bed and items of medical equipment could be seen at the bedside.

As they approached, Floyd realised that a patient was in the bed accompanied by a stern-looking nurse, a tall man in pin striped trousers and tails together with two official-looking sorts.

'Mr Carter,' announced Thomas in earshot of the whole group, 'I'd like to introduce you to Mr Paul Aldridge. Our Trustee.'

The heads of the party turned to greet the new arrivals as Thomas and Floyd presented themselves to the Trustee. Standing at the end of the bed, which had been tilted at the top and bottom to place the Trustee in a partially sitting position, Thomas made formal introductions to all.

Paul Aldridge was a tall man, now reduced to a waif-like form wrapped in a thick silk gown. He was wearing a brilliant white panama hat and rested his right hand on a gentleman's walking stick. His features were gaunt and frail with small wisps of white thin hair escaping from under his hat – the chemo having removed all but a few strands. But there was something about him, tugging in Floyd's mind something that made him feel familiar.

'Floyd, Thomas,' the man spoke in a dry husky voice, 'I'm so please that you have been able to see me. 'I just regret that it is under such sad circumstances.' Pausing for a moment reflecting on his own words, he continued waving his hand up and down in front of himself.

'Not this, not my condition, I've had a long and full life. No it's what happened to Doreen and Li Wei that gives me such a heavy heart.'

Paul turned to the butler raising his right hand.

'Please Jenkins, would you mind pulling the chairs over for Thomas and Floyd and then if we could have some privacy it would be much appreciated?'

'Actually, sir,' said Thomas, 'perhaps it would be better if I leave the two of you to talk alone.'

'Very good, Thomas,' said the Trustee, as Thomas returned to the house leaving Floyd alone to speak with one of the world's most powerful men. A man who didn't have much time left in this world.

# Thirty one

It was warm in the helicopter's cabin and as the huge aircraft descended from the sky to kiss the Aberdeenshire soil Becca was filled with anticipation in equal measure with the dread of what else she might find. The last few inches before touching down she peered through the window watching the long course grass of the park land fan out as a swirling cushion of air billowed out beneath them.

As she stooped to run away from the downdraught a young Athena agent came forward to meet her. Every inch a soldier, Lance had recently joined the Unit having made quite a reputation for himself in military intelligence. Briefing Becca on the intercepted police radio message it appeared that a suspicious road traffic accident had occurred very close to where they had been able to triangulate the source of a recent call to Yvette's mobile telephone.

'Just take me there.' She snapped, clearly in no mood for small talk. Becca had wasted no time after leaving the facility in Chobham in running a personnel scan for a suitable deputy. The events over the past week had affected her a lot more than she had realised. Normally she possessed clarity of thought but she had realised how much she had allowed her emotions to cloud her focus even to the point of planning a future with Floyd together with her at Athena; her confidant, her partner … *Don't you see Becca we can make a difference here do some good in the world* … sometimes it is the smallest of things that tell us just how wrong we have been – and so it was that moment when she was speaking with Floyd that the ideas and thoughts that she had allowed to coalesce into an idealised fantasy were dismissed by him in his annoyingly superior manner.

A worm in her gut gnawed deeper.

Well, she concluded, if that's the way he wants it he's on his own.

The freight park surprised Becca, it was certainly away out on its own, but all the same very easy to get to and nestled in a hollow surrounded on two sides by rich green woodland which, even in the poor weather that was soaking her and her agents to the core, was a place of beauty and solitude. She could imagine living in a place like this – plenty of space to think. Resurfacing again the reality of the ugliness that inhabited this place began to reveal itself. Having searched a number of the units littering the site Lance eventually located the right freight container severing the U bolt on the padlock with industrial bolt cutters.

As the doors opened it was immediately obvious that they had found them as the vapid odour poured out from within.

Within the hour all of the captives had been removed and emergency first aid administered where it was required. Hydration was the immediate issue and as the Grampian Ambulance Service began to arrive en mass, the ambulances bouncing through the potholes filled with muddy water, the Athena team took their leave instructing Scott Cooper, the ACC, directly to coordinate the follow up response.  ·

'Please,' said the young dark-haired woman, 'please will you contact my parents and let them know that I'm alive?'

Becca turned to her, she looked at the young lady sat on a pile of rubble wrapped in an emergency blanket. She had suffered great cruelty it was clear but there was a certain authority in her voice. Normally Becca would leave the victim support work to others, but she felt strangely compelled to approach the girl.

'Hello,' she said in a gentle voice, 'have the medics seen you yet?'

'No, the others are in greater need than me,' she paused to pull the blanket further around her, 'I'll be OK, but would you do that for me, call my parents?'

'I really should leave that to the Police..'

The girl interrupted. 'Really?' she said quizzically. 'From what I see you are the person in charge around here and you can do what you like.'

For the second time that day Becca realised just how far she had started to doubt herself and allow herself to be subordinated to others. It took this pitiful young girl to speak a few naïve words which carried with them great truth to bring her to her senses. She was the Commander of Athena and was answerable to nobody. She turned her head away from the girl in the direction of the first ambulance team.

'Medic.' She barked so ferociously that there was no question of her being challenged.

As the paramedic trotted towards them she took a single step back to let him attend to the girl.

'What's your name?' Becca enquired as the paramedic opened his equipment case.

'Oksana.' She replied, 'I live in Kiev ...'

# Thirty two

Floyd and Thomas sat together in the restaurant of the facility enjoying one of many such meals that they had shared together over the week that Floyd had been staying there. They spoke companionably as they finished up, a young waiter cleared the table and brought out coffee allowing them to read their newspapers in peace.

Floyd had been scanning all of the news articles voraciously following the dramatic events that had unfolded in Aberdeenshire with the successful release of five captives of the slave gang. It was on all of the news channels for a couple of days, but was quickly overtaken by other global events, dramas and economic crises. The local Aberdeen Press and Journal website provided more extended commentary but at the end of the day despite all of the coverage, interviews and vox pops, nobody was really saying anything and there was definitely no mention of Athena who, it was clear to Floyd, had made the breakthrough. The ACC, Scott Cooper deftly positioned himself as the man of the hour also paying tribute to Sergeant Lachlan Anderson who died in tragic circumstances while pursuing his enquiries into the case.

'Can you believe this rubbish?' Floyd remarked partly in frustration, partly amused. He passed the article to Thomas.

'Ah, yes, well it's good news alright; I see Ms Atworth's fingerprints all over this. I've also been in touch with some of our intelligence officers who have been scanning activities by other, shall we say, less savoury parts of the Foundation. It seems there has been a bit of a break through on securing the encryption algorithm that they have been using.'

'Thomas you must take this to Paul, he'll want to do something about this.' And then more reflectively he said. 'You know, Thomas, I must admit that I was truly sceptical to start with, but the more that I have spoken with him over the last week I now see that you were right, he really is a man of integrity.'

'It's true,' said Thomas, 'he will want to do something, but we will have to be careful, I am sure the last thing that we need at the moment is all out conflict with another Trustee; the geopolitical landscape is already very fragile at the moment.' He folded up the newspaper rising from his chair.

'And now Mr Carter, if you'll excuse me I have ...' But he didn't have the chance to finish his sentence. Jenkins ran into the room flustered pushing his black hair back over his head with his left hand as he supported himself with his right hand on the back of a chair in an effort to recover his breath.

'Gentleman, please you must come, its Trustee Aldridge.'

'What is it?' Demanded Thomas.

'Please just come.'


The three of them walked briskly down the hallway of the medical wing. As they approached the Trustee's room Jenkins stood to one side of the entrance and held the door open for Floyd and Thomas to enter.

The Trustee lay motionless in his hospital bed which had been positioned directly in front of the picture window overlooking the formal gardens. Inside the room the bright overhead fluorescent light buzzed loudly bathing everything in its artificial light. Outside the grey skies brooded, clouds hanging low in the sky and the windows started to speckle with rain.

The nurse rounded the bed touching Thomas gently on the arm. 'He passed away just moments ago, Thomas.' Turning to Floyd, she coolly said. 'This was next to him, it's for you. He asked me to give it to you when the time came.'

It was completely dark outside as Thomas entered into the drawing room. He walked to the windows and released the long purple velvet curtains from the chords and drew them together shutting out the night.

'Here, I think you need this.' Thomas said pouring a glass of whisky from a fine cut crystal decanter. Floyd took it with a nod of gratitude.

He was listening to the Dictaphone that the nurse had passed to him earlier in the day. He'd probably already listened to it a dozen times by now.

'... *Floyd you've learned so much over these past days about things that are both seen and unseen, the world is not always how it appears. But it appears to people how it is meant to appear; not how it is.*

*I would dearly love for this world to be a better place but sometimes we have to play the deck that we are dealt with. When my father died I inherited this position and this duty – I didn't have to, but I accepted it and to this day I know that it was the right thing to do.*

*Now it is your turn. Listen to Thomas, he will give you wise counsel.*

*And remember life is not black and white. I am afraid to say that many well intentioned people and organisations polarise the world into good and bad. That is a mistake. Remember that in all good things there is an element of bad and in all bad things some good.*

*Floyd, it's your turn now – if you accept the Foundation you will be the new Trustee – Please make it your mission to make the world a better place...'*

'Here's to Paul.' Said Floyd as they toasted him.

'You know, Floyd, I truly do hope you accept the Trusteeship but Paul's right, Athena will never accept the Foundation, and that means Ms Atworth, too. I hope you realise.

# Thirty three

Ten days later

Nobody ever sees a bag lady, even in the middle of the daytime a reminder of the ills in our society – perhaps. More likely we fear that fate may roll the dice again and find ourselves the destitute ones. Better to pretend she's not there at all.

Had people noticed then they would have spotted her today on Union Grove pushing her grubby tartan trolley over the uneven paving stones. She had been here before a few weeks ago watching the very same flat noticing the activities of the highly strung girl, the young man and also the bald-headed Slavic man who broke in that time.

Hobbling up to the front door of the apartment block she slipped her hand into the pocket of the tartan trolley and pulled out a lock pick; within seconds she was in the building.

Quickly the woman made her way up the stairs no longer stooping, but instead a nimble figure, curious looking in the ragged clothes. Again she picked the lock to the apartment and closed the door behind her. Securing the door with the deadbolt she then removed the wig and tatty coat that she had been wearing, placing them in the tartan trolley after removing the explosive device – her reason for being there. She made her way to the bedroom, opened a drawer beneath the bed and placed the device carefully inside making space among the sheets. Having set the contacts and primed the device it was set to go off the moment somebody entered the bedroom.

Wasting no time the woman stood in the middle of the apartment carefully looking around her making sure that she hadn't moved anything that would give away her visit. Satisfied she retrieved the tartan trolley and left the building. The moment she reached the street there was a white van waiting for her with the side door open. She passed the trolley up to the unseen person in the back of the van, and then got in herself slamming the door shut as the van lurched forward with a slight wheel spin; it then sped down the road disappearing from view around the next corner.

'Did everything go to plan, Smith?' asked a surly woman's voice.

'Yes, Commander, everything is set, just as you instructed.

Floyd passed a slice of cake over the side of his cubicle to Archie relieved that he hadn't spilt any of his coffee in the process.

'Cheers, Floyd,' he said 'so what is it, your birthday or something?' Archie asked happy for the excuse to take a break from his spreadsheet. 'You've certainly got your appetite back after being off sick, mate.'

'No nothing like that, just been running through some of the bills with the partner, whose being a real pain in the arse. You know, giving me grief over my recoveries. So … I thought I'd give myself a little treat – I mean, if I don't then nobody else will right?'

Archie sat there unable to speak having put the whole slice of cake into his mouth.

'So you up to much this weekend Archie? Going out with Duggie and his pals?'

Washing down the cake with the dregs in his coffee mug Archie cleared his mouth.

'I expect so, probably hit a couple of bars first, perhaps a curry then to a club. Dae ye wannae join us? Sorry 'bout your girlfriend bailing out on you's, mate. Might get lucky if you come out eh?'

'You know what, Arch', I think I will,' said Floyd. It seemed as if life at Baker Smith and Clarkwell was getting back to normal he thought.

Sitting back down in his cubicle Floyd busied himself shuffling through his papers glancing at the clock in the bottom right hand corner of his computer monitor. Four fifteen, only ten minutes after he last looked. Friday afternoons always seemed to last an age he reflected. It was then he noticed that he had received an email five minutes ago from "A Friend".

A sense of Deja vu made Floyd consider pinching himself to check this was real, not some weird Groundhog moment. Click, he launched the email.

Floyd – you need to see this.

And just like last time the text of the email was followed by a link to a web page.

Holy shit, not again he thought. He clicked the forward button on the toolbar and sent the email to his personal email address. Anything like the last one, he thought, and HR will have a field day.

He sat back in his chair leaning against the back rest tilting it slightly backwards. Realising that his heart rate had started racing he rubbed his eyes and the bridge of his nose taking a few deep breaths seeking to calm himself down.

'Come on, Floyd, get a grip.' He said to himself. Immediately the phone on his desk rang demanding his attention.

Hesitating for just a moment Floyd lifted the receiver just before the call would divert to voice mail.

'H … Hello, Floyd Carter speaking!'

'Mr Carter, it's Thomas here, I'm so sorry to call you at your work.'

'Thomas, you said that you wouldn't contact me during the period of administration. It's probably best that we don't speak until Tuesday, I'll give you an answer then. I'd really like to just work through this on my own OK.'

'I completely understand that, Floyd, but that's not why I'm calling,' he started. 'Did you receive my email, there's something there that you need to see. It's important, Floyd, just click on the link, watch the footage and I'll stay on the line.'

Floyd opened the email again and this time didn't hesitate in clicking through to the web feed.

It took him a few moments to realise that the grainy image was of his apartment on Union Grove viewed from a corner of the living area.

'I must apologize Floyd, this must seem like a gross intrusion of your privacy, we had a small web cam installed into one of the movement detectors of your alarm system ... are you watching?'

'Yes, Thomas, who is that, what are they doing? Then a moment later he said. 'Thomas, actually I think I've met that woman before. The image isn't great but I think she is one of the crew that met Becca and me at the farmhouse over near Ardoe. What's she doing?

'I'm afraid that makes complete sense, Floyd, what she has planted into your apartment is an explosive device ... it seems Athena has decided that you're a loose end and need tidying up. It's obviously too dangerous for you to go home Floyd ... would you like me to contact the Police and get the Bomb squad on site to sort this out?'

Floyd's mouth was dry; he was finding it hard to marshal his thoughts. Moments passed, all Floyd could see in his mind's eye was the woman walking into his bedroom planting the bomb.

'*... Athena are going to be all over the Foundation so you need to choose sides, it's all or nothing.*'

Those were her words, he remembered them now, *all or nothing*. How could he have been so blind? This is exactly what the Trustee had said – that she would see this as black and white, and if he is not with her then he is against her. He clenched his fist in anger, snapping his pencil in his grip. In his ear he could hear Thomas ... 'Mr Carter, are you there, are you alright?'

So that's how she wants it, trying to draw first blood. Well if that's the way she wants it ...

'Thomas, I'm here ... I'm OK, now listen very carefully ...'

'Yes, Mr Carter?'

'Thomas, I'm in. I accept, I will be the next Trustee.' He declared and then hung up.

Floyd sat motionless for an age. Coming to his senses he realised that Archie was peering over the top of the cubicle wall.

'Mate, tell me if I'm being nosey, but I couldn't help catching some of what you were saying on the phone just now. Sounds like you were talking to a recruitment agent. Bet you were, Floyd ... have you got yoursel' a new job?

'You know what Archie... I think I have!'

# Epilogue

Ten months later

The young man behind the concierge desk at the Grand Hotel in St Moritz snapped his fingers at the bell boy further along the corridor.

'Quick,' he said to the junior, 'that's Mr Carter. Go and open the door for him. Schnell!'

Happy once more that one of the Hotel's more important VIP's had been properly treated he reopened his newspaper to where he had left off:

*Die Neue Zurcher Zeitung*

*Police were called in to investigate the mysterious death of Texan Charles Illingworth, the secretive billionaire from Fort Worth.*

*His body was found by staff at the legendary Grand Hotel in St Moritz yesterday morning after guests complained of a disturbance in one of the VIP suites on the eighth floor. Police have been slow to release any specific information but have now appealed for witnesses.*

*Despite a lack of official comment a member of the hotel staff has broken ranks and spoken with the press under conditions of anonymity saying that the deceased had clearly been subjected to physical torture and apparently had also shown signs of having been branded with red hot irons leaving a very distinctive mark on his skin. No further details were forthcoming.*

*A police spokesman has commented that the victim's next of kin have been informed, but insisted that they would take no further questions at this morning's press briefing when pressed by freelance journalist, Rebecca Atworth.*

Coming soon…

*The Winepress*

# Prologue

Spring 1947 – Blackmoor Copse, Wiltshire

When he turned the valve down on the paraffin lantern beside his bed, slowly descending the alcove into gloom, he was blissfully ignorant of the events that would begin to unfold there in his cottage a few short hours after he would slip into unconscious slumber.

In his bed Barry turned to gaze into the hearth of the fire place of the single roomed Gamekeeper's cottage, cherishing the glow of the dying embers as they cast dancing shadows reaching out from the simple stick furniture, the shot gun cartridges on the table and Alfie's twitching ears; his geriatric gun dog. As the shadows danced their jig on the thick stone walls of the cottage Barry felt the tingle of contentment in his belly: So far from the smouldering battlefields that he had left behind in Europe a few short years ago. All just a memory now, the simple life and existence of a Gamekeeper had worked wonders for Barry's scarred mind – He surrendered himself to sleep's soft embrace.

They came out of nowhere, silently slipping through the unlocked door and quickly coshing the rousing canine before he gave away their presence to the sole inhabitant who was their real target. The blow to the beast was sharp and surgical, knocking him out cold but with no real lasting damage. There were three of them occupying the small space within the cottage. They were dressed in darkened military fatigues, blackened faces, and absolute focus. The lead figure ducked out of the front door and with a silent gesture to an unseen party beckoned a fourth person into the cramped surroundings that Barry Kent called home.

Unlike the soldiers the fourth man was a painfully thin and wiry character, and were Barry awake to see him in the dim light as he approached he would have seen an intelligent face displaying a complete detachment as it peered down at him just as if he were a specimen in an experiment, a laboratory rat or a bug in a Petri dish. For indeed, that is exactly what he was.

The scientist beckoned to a soldier with a nod who stepped fluidly over to the bedside. He reached out with both of his hands placing them over Barry's face in readiness to subdue him while the Scientist adeptly administered a fast acting cocktail of sedatives directly into his subject's Carotid Artery. As it was there was no need for the soldier's precaution, and within moments Barry slid even beyond his deep sleep and further into the void of a chemically induced coma.

"Thank you gentlemen," the Scientist said in his clipped voice, "we can relax a little now. Mr. Kent here will not be aware of anything for at least other five or six hours. Plenty of time!" He adjusted his small round glasses on his nose as he considered his next steps.

"Captain," he hailed to the group's leader, "I would be obliged if you and your men would build up the fire. In order to secure the best results for incubation, we need it to be a lot warmer in here."

"Yes Sir!" Retorted the Captain.

The Scientist returned to his subject and digging into his medical bag retrieved a syringe followed by a vial full of a golden brown coloured liquid. After slipping on rubber gloves he swiftly went about the business of drawing the required dose into the syringe and, taking care to expel any air bubbles, plunging the needle into the upper arm of the subject.

They spent another hour in the Gamekeeper's cottage maintaining an optimal environment and ensuring the subject was comfortable, all the while being careful to ensure that they had left behind no trace of having been there. Eventually the Scientist removed the gloves that sheathed his hands with a flourish of gusto and snapped. "Right, we're done here I'll write up my report in the morning, but first please take me up to The Grange, I know Lord Stephens is keen to be immediately appraised.

"Y' Sir," replied the second in command who quickly shepherded the men out into the dark silent woods. A short walk and an even shorter drive later and The Scientist had been delivered into the care of the butler at The Grange ready to deliver his debrief.

The inky black sky had prevented The Scientist from fully absorbing the size and grandeur of The Grange, which was Lord Stephens' residence while in the West Country. However, once in the hallway he could see from the huge circular space and twin staircases tracing the curvature of the wall that Lord Stephens was clearly a man who would expect and get whatever it was that he wanted.

"This way please," instructed the tall dark haired butler, who was immaculately turned out despite the hour, "I'll put you in the billiard room, His Lordship will be with you shortly."

"Thank you." Responded the Scientist making an effort to remain aloof, but battling with the sense of intimidation that his betters always inflicted upon him.

He paced across to the other side of the room and facing the large ceiling to floor sash window he gazed out thoughtfully at a few dim lights twinkling in the nearby village windows and the dark blue silhouette of trees in an otherwise completely dark landscape.

"Ah, Thompson," boomed a voice from the doorway, causing The Scientist, Andrew Thompson, to jump with a start, "is it done?"

"Yes Lord Stephens it all went off perfectly, just like we planned", he stumbled, his heart now pounding in his chest, "A... and I agree he seems the perfect subject for trial, good physical condition so in my expert opinion the pathogen has a very good chance of naturalising in the host."

"Good, good you've done well, now just a couple of pieces of housekeeping; firstly do you have the research file?"

"Yes Sir, it's all right here in my bag."

"No copies that might get out in the open anywhere are there, can't take chances you know with something as delicate as this? Asked his Lordship in as amiable a manner as he could summon.

"No Sir," responded Thompson, feeling more confident and allowing his pompous nature to show once more, "Only those people who matter know anything about this now Sir, and you can rely on me to be the absolute sole of discretion."

"Oh I know I can," sneered Lord Stephens.

It took Thompson a moment to register the menace in the peer's voice. Had he had the time he would have been able to feel confused by the sudden change in the peer's demeanour, and why on earth was His Lordship now levelling a pistol aimed at his chest? The last observation that The Scientist made during his lifetime was the muzzle flash of the pistol held by the peer who was clad in a dark brown shirt, and then ... nothing.

# One

Bedford Road, Aberdeen – current day

It had been three months since Seth had submitted his application for funding to the Research Council without even having received an acknowledgment from them – and now this. He thrust the letter into the pocket of his brown corduroy jacket fuming under his breath over the three sentences he had just read on his door step.

Pushing the old Javelin racing bike with drop handle bars through the front door Dr Seth Wylie tried in vain to put it out of his mind determined not to be late again for his undergraduates' tutorial.

The bicycle had seen better days, in its prime it was bright red and the rider had a choice of ten derailleur gears. Today as Seth struggled along Bedford Road his pride and joy had become weather worn to a rusty orange and the choice of working gears now limited to only three, but that suited him just fine. As he pedaled faster he could feel his pulse starting to race, it felt good on that cold March morning, a tinge of frost still caressing the grassy verge and around the edges of puddles in the road's many potholes. As Seth made progress towards the University he would catch glimpses of the sea to his right littered with supply vessels making the tide.

*"...We thank you for your application for funding in support of your research into the genetic markers for varying*

*human characteristics in support of which you have provided impressive empirical observation relating to the impact of genetics in both racial groupings and behaviours. However, it is clear to us that there will be strict ethical concerns surrounding any such research, and so it is incumbent upon us to refer this file to the Ethics Committee for consideration before we can advance further this application.*

*We fully anticipate that there will be a requirement on all such research to be moderated by a committee appointed mentor as a minimum requirement for Council funding to ensure strict ethical probity...."*

Seth stood up on his peddles pounding away faster driving the frustration out of him as the biting wind whipped his lanky dirty blond hair. He yanked the handle bars to the right narrowly missing oncoming traffic and sailed down the slope past the vast glass cube which is the main Library and skidding to a stop at the bike racks outside the oppressive 1970's building which housed the research labs that Seth called home.

Seth walked through the main door and past the lecture halls where as a fresh undergraduate he had started along his journey of discovery into the code that defines life itself and how it dictates the makeup of each and every one of us. Running up the stairs, now taking them two at a time, he past the faculty offices which he moved into a couple of years ago having earned a reputation for being a brilliant academic and researcher, albeit hampered in today's world by being chronically disorganised and not in the least business minded. But for all that Seth was happy.

The tutorial room was already full with his Thursday morning tutor group, five fresh faced first years, all smiling and greeting the apologetic shambling Doctor as he lurched in and plonked heavily down in his seat. Seth unhooked his battered leather satchel and rifled through the cluttered contents, eventually locating the elusive item – an eCigarette.

"Sorry people," He started as he crossed his legs and while resting an elbow on his knee he sharply drew in breath through the cigarette substitute.

"Um, so where were we last week, did we finish the section on DNA polymerase I and its ability to hydrolyse DNA chains under certain conditions?" And so the session began, the students loved him, not because he was a great teacher, he was too scatterbrained to be a good communicator, but because he was so human and insightful about his area of expertise. Seth completely forgot the morning post and enjoyed the banter with his young followers.

It wasn't until lunchtime as he we reclining at his desk that he was reminded of the letter. His office was adjacent to the post grad research laboratory. Measuring about ten feet by fifteen it was pokey at best and after squeezing Seth's desk, a mass of books strewn across the wall of shelves, his various molecular models made from red, black and white balls – there was very little room for anything else.

A vibration alerted him to his mobile phone which was now ringing. It appeared to be coming from somewhere on his desk but finding it was going to be a challenge.

"Come on where are you? Why do you always do this to me?" He frantically searched for the phone, only locating it the moment the called bounced to voicemail.

"You coming down to the faculty meeting Seth?" A woman's voice chirped from the door. It was Elspeth his post grad student, petite with severely short black cropped hair; he thoroughly enjoyed his role as her counsellor for her PhD research. "Think we'll be running through the Easter vacation staffing shouldn't be much else going on."

"Thanks Elspeth," he replied retrieving his phone and scrolling through to missed calls, "would you mind standing in for me?" She was his right hand whenever it came to administration, for which he was eternally grateful. He gave her his best cheesy grin as his call connected – Elspeth gave him the thumbs up and retreated back into the lab.

"Oh hi Love," Seth started, "sorry lost my phone there for a moment. How's it going?" He asked absentmindedly, his left hand toying with a metallic Newton's cradle on the window ledge. Trying to release two balls at the side one after the other he fiddled around when suddenly the resulting motion of the balls causing a loud clattering in the confined space.

"What on earth was that?" Asked Angela. It was less a question and more an admonishment.

"Whoops, my bad!" Said Seth clamping his hand over the toy bringing the sound and motion to an abrupt stop. "Everything OK?"

"Yes, all's well," she replied, "it's just that I was talking again this morning with one of the associates and we got chatting more about all that stuff that you do in the lab and what not, and well he agrees that you should be doing something to get some value out of it."

It was a long running conversation between Seth and his girlfriend, Angela, and the source of a great deal of frustration to both parties.

Angela worked in a large commercial law office in the west end of the city and ever since running a case involving intellectual property rights she was convinced that Seth was selling himself short leading the life of a crusty academic. Angela liked to spend time chatting up one of the IP associates, a real mover and shaker, and a bit of a dish too, she thought. Why couldn't Seth be a little bit more driven like him?

"Well anyway Dean has said that he'll look into it. If you wanted we can catch up with him after work, or I can do it on my own if you like, I'll swing by yours later to update you. How does that sound?"

Seth scanned the surfaces looking for somewhere to put his executive toy, and suddenly realised that he had not really been paying much attention to what Angela had been saying. "OK love that sounds great, see you later maybe." He hung up, his attention once again on the metal toy as it was then that he noticed the inch square Post It stuck to the base. At first glimpse he couldn't decipher the hastily scribbled words until turning it around it became legible. Seeing the name that had been written on the Post-It sent a thrill of excitement shuddering through him, he had to stop himself from jumping up and down – *come on Seth you're not a child any longer.* And it was then he also noticed the date noted on the yellow sticky being two days ago.

"Damn and blast," he muttered, "hope he still wants to speak?" Flipping open his phone Seth concentrated hard on getting the international access number correct as he hurriedly punched the digits into his telephone. He sat bolt upright at his desk as the speaker clicked and whirred making connections through wires and fibre and all manner of gadgetry, eventually rewarding him with a ringing tone. And then again, and again.

*"Hej, detta ar professor Lindstroms kontor."* Came the woman's voice.

"Oh, yes um," blustered Seth, "I'm sorry I'm British...," well no, that's not what I mean I'm quite happy being British, but..er.. what I'm trying to say is that I ..um..can't speak Swedish, so would you mind speaking English, er..please?"

"Oh of course sir, you must be Dr Wylie, I was expecting your call a couple of days ago!" She paused for a moment.

"It's a pity you hadn't called back sooner, only my Father has just been admitted to hospital for a scheduled procedure on his throat so he will be out of action for a little while, and he was hoping to speak with you." Her English was excellent albeit with a slight hint of Nordic cadence.

"It is nothing serious Dr, and I am sure that my Father will make a terrible patient for those poor doctors and nurses, but he will be over the effects of the.., how do you say...the anesthetic, in a day or two. In fact I shall be going there tomorrow morning to take his computer. Of course, he won't be talking for a while so he will be emailing us once he is able to sit up. You will no doubt hear from him very soon."

Seth could have kicked himself, how could he have missed such a chance to speak with the world famous geneticist Arne Lindstrom. "So would you happen to know what it was that Professor Lindstrom wanted to speak to me about?" He ventured.

"Oh forgive me Doctor Wylie, I thought you must have known, but my Father has been nominated by your funding body to act as your mentor for your proposed research project. It seems that the funding will be jointly provided partly by the Council and partly by another governmental laboratory in the South of England who has been made aware of your research."

Seth felt uncertain that he could believe such good luck following the missive he'd received just that morning.

"That's... that's marvelous he gushed. But when will I get some sort of formal notice?" His mind was now racing over the mountain of paperwork that he would no doubt need to grapple with to get this pinned down – not his strong subject, he wondered for a moment if he should call Elspeth to help him out.

"Don't worry about that Dr Whylie, my Father has asked me to assist you with all such practical matters – it's what I do best. All you need to worry about right now is getting to the joint venture research laboratory to start on Monday. I'll email you with all of the necessary details and organise your travel arrangements. OK?"

"Sure, yes... fine that sounds great... wonderful even," Seth's head was spinning and unable to marshal his thoughts. "One thing though, who and where is this research establishment?"

Ms Lindstrom paused; Seth could hear her clicking on the keypad of her computer. "Here it is," she announced, "it's called the Porton Down Research Centre and it appears to be near to the city of Salisbury in Wiltshire... and, oh yes...it's a research establishment for the Ministry of Defence!"

# Two

The Grand Hotel, St Moritz

Just for an instant as he stepped in the lift compartment Floyd forgot all about the great responsibility that was his to carry, a man charged with leading a globally diverse organisation supplying the needs to a large part of the world's population. Never a moment to stop, to still his mind and remind himself of who he really was.

However, in that moment as he stared vacantly through the open doors of the ornately panelled lift compartment, he gazed at his reflection in the half length mirror opposite above the exquisite Louis XVI rosewood display table bearing a tasteful floral spray. The young man he saw was no longer wearing a fifty thousand dollar suit instead he was looking back at Floyd through the eyes of a twenty eight year old, average physique and the whiff of grey brushed over his ears sporting jeans and a supermarket bought tee shirt, a slightly hangdog expression. It seemed to Floyd so long ago that he was that person, having since immersed himself into his new life. What he did, was not a job, oh no, not even a career – it was his calling. And while at first he doubted himself he knew now that this was who he was and what he was destined to be.

That was then, some three years ago – and as the compartment to the lift closed the inside mirrors on the closing doors revealed him again as he is now, a more mature and toned version of the man outside, a shock of white hair combed back in that sophisticated European way and every inch the man in charge. Floyd Carter is the sole Trustee and Chairman of *"The Foundation."*

Stepping into the luxurious executive suite on the eighth floor of the hotel, Floyd took a few short paces though the elegant hallway and into the main living area of his living quarters. The apartment occupied more than quarter of the entire eighth floor of this super exclusive hotel. The opulence was amazing and the view of St Moritz and the Alps beyond through the huge glass walls simply breathtaking, but it was the two men standing before him backs to the contemporary fireplace with flames licking up the chimney in the centre of the room, that consumed his attention.

They stood there unmoving in a posture of two soldiers standing at ease before their commanding officer. Everything about the two appeared identical. The twins both Israelis previously in the employ of Mossad, had cropped black hair and wore smart navy blue suits, fuchsia pink shirts left open at the neck and while the suits were styled by some of the best tailors it is always difficult to fully disguise a holstered pistol.

The two dark haired men both in their mid-thirties relaxed as Floyd raised a hand and with a sweeping gesture said. "Please Noam, Ariel do sit down. It's been a long day. I'm going to fix myself a drink, please carry on with your report."

Floyd stepped towards the cabinet and poured a small measure of whisky into a large crystal tumbler. "Can I get either of you anything?" He smirked knowing that not a drop of alcohol had ever passed either of their lips and probably never would.

It was Noam who spoke first as was normally the case. While the two men were physically identical in every way down to the last gene on their twenty third pair of chromosomes, they couldn't be more different in how they conducted themselves. Noam did most of the talking, that's not to say that Ariel never talked, it's just Noam always knew what he was going to say most of the time and so he felt the world would be a better place without more words and no more meaning. When Ariel spoke… it was wise to listen very carefully.

Their parents had named them with great insight for Noam was always pleasant and kind a friend to everyone, and Ariel was moody and silent, never at rest like a prowling lion. But the characteristic that they had in common and in abundance was an unswerving loyalty to their cause and a willingness to carry out unspeakable acts of barbarity to please their superiors.

Floyd sipped the fiery liquid with a gasp of pure pleasure as the Glenfiddich Reserve reached all the way down into him. Fixing them with a steely gaze he issued a one word instruction.

"Report?"